Suddenly the Creature Pulled Its Head Back and Snapped Its Eyes Open.

Whipping its head back into the hole, it turned, blocking the entrance with its body. From inside came a thin, high-pitched wail.

The three Monster Hunters looked at one another.

"Casey?" said Brian softly. Then he called lustily, "Casey Rogoff, are you in there?"

"Yes," came a prompt but faint reply, and Numbles almost cheered aloud. . . .

"Hi, Casey," Numbles called. "Are you okay? I mean, are you hurt or anything? Did the . . . the animal hurt you?"

"No, it didn't hurt me," Casey said indignantly. "But it won't let me go. I tried to run away, but it wouldn't let me."

"You don't think," Brian asked Numbles in a soft voice, "that it wants to eat her?"

Weekly Reader Book Club Presents

MYSTERY OF THE KIDNAPPED KIDNAPPER

Nancy
Garden

PUBLISHED BY POCKET BOOKS

New York London Toronto Sydney Tokyo Singapore

This book is a presentation of Newfield Publications, Inc.
Newfield Publications offers book clubs for children from
preschool through high school. For further information
write to: **Newfield Publications, Inc.,**
4343 Equity Drive, Columbus, Ohio 43228.

Published by arrangement with Pocket Books,
a division of Simon & Schuster Inc.
Newfield Publications is a federally registered trademark
of Newfield Publications, Inc.
Weekly Reader is a federally registered trademark
of Weekly Reader Corporation.

A MINSTREL PAPERBACK *ORIGINAL*

A Minstrel Book published by
POCKET BOOKS, a division of Simon & Schuster Inc.
1230 Avenue of the Americas, New York, NY 10020

Front cover illustration by Jeffrey Lindberg

ISBN: 0-671-76008-4

Printed in the U.S.A.

For the Camp-In Kids
and Staff
and
for Champ

CONTENTS

AUTHOR'S NOTE

Most of this story is made up, but legend and popular belief say that both Lake Champlain and Loch Ness are home to lake monsters. And the Boston Museum of Science does hold Camp-Ins regularly.

One of the best things about being an author is that you sometimes get to go to exciting places. To write this book, I had to go to Lake Champlain and to a Boston Museum of Science Camp-In. Much of what I've said about the Science Museum is true, as you'll find if you go there, but a good deal is made up. I've had to change the layout some, so don't expect to find the Great Reptiles exhibit, or an extension of the Wave Tank, or windows with loose gratings, or a heating and air-conditioning duct coming out in the rain forest exhibit, or the corridor to which Numbles was taken.

My thanks go to Marianne Dunne, who directs the Camp-In program, which is truly wonderful, to Carolyn Kirdahy, a museum librarian, to all the friendly museum staffers and guards whose names I don't know, and to the Brownie Scout from Maine whose pleasure at the Omni show during the Camp-In added considerably to my own.

Nancy Garden
Carlisle, MA

We the undersigned, being of sound mind and body, hereby swear to keep open minds in the face of all unexplained and unsolved crimes, believing that there are ancient and monstrous creatures still in the world, capable of inflicting harm and imparting terror. And we further pledge that, as Monster Hunters, we will track down all such beings that come to our attention, and see that Justice is done.

....

(Signed)

THE CREATURE

IT'LL BE DARK SOON, Numbles—Edward Crane, Jr., on his school records—realized, glancing out the window as his bus approached Boston. It's a good thing Kevin said the Science Museum is open late on Fridays.

Numbles took out his friend Kevin Rogoff's letter to read for the tenth time:

Dear Num,

You've got to come to Boston over Veterans Day (Mom and Dad say it's okay). There's an awesome exhibit at the Science Museum. You've got to see it! It's called the Great Reptiles and it's this huge display, with models of weird creatures that look like dinosaurs. There are even a couple of live creatures that are descended from the ancient ones. But here's the best part. *There's one live one no one can identify!*

Mom says we can all go to the museum Friday night as soon as your bus gets in. The museum's open till nine. My little sister Casey's going on something called a Camp-In there with her Brownie troop that night, and we've got to drop her off. (Those lucky kids get to spend the night in the museum!) You and I get to go back the next day, though, to pick Casey up. . . .

The rest of the letter was about what Kevin had done since school had started that fall. It was pretty boring, except for what he said about his pet eastern smooth green snake (*Opheodrys vernalis*). Numbles had a pretty good collection of reptiles and amphibians himself at home in Grove Hill, Vermont. His favorites were a snapping turtle named Rosey and a Texas horned lizard (*Phrynosoma cornutum*) that his uncle Fred had sent him from Arizona. Uncle Fred was a herpetologist—an expert on reptiles and amphibians. Numbles was going to be one, too. Kevin wasn't, but, Numbles thought, at least he figured out how much I want to see that unidentified reptile!

The bus finally pulled into the station in downtown

Boston. Numbles spotted Kevin right away. His slight figure looked almost large next to the little blond pig-tailed girl beside him.

Numbles, who was as plump as Kevin was skinny, impatiently waited his turn to get off the bus. The sooner they got going, the more time they'd have at the museum.

Six-year-old Casey Rogoff was quiet on the way to the museum, snuggled into a corner of the backseat with a backpack and a big plastic garbage bag containing, Kevin explained, her bedding. But as soon as Kevin's parents dropped the three of them off, Casey shouldered the bag and her backpack, which was so covered with dinosaur stickers that Numbles could barely see its fabric. "Okay," she said, turning to the boys. "You can go away now. Goodbye. I'll see you tomorrow."

"No way, José," Kevin said, grabbing her. He steered her through the doors leading into the museum, which was huge, with six floors, two wings, a planetarium, and several theaters. "Mom said for me to take you to your Brownie leader," said Kevin. "Besides, if I know you, you'll get lost if I don't." He turned to Numbles. "Casey has gotten lost thirteen times in her life," he said with a stern glance at his sister. "Since she's only six, that's an average of two point one-six-six-six times a year."

Numbles grinned. Kevin liked math the way he himself liked reptiles, and the way Casey, if her backpack was any indication, seemed to like dinosaurs.

It took another few minutes to locate Casey's Brownie leader and troop. By then the museum's vast lobby was swarming with some three hundred excited little girls lugging garbage bags like Casey's or rolled-up sleeping bags. They were being shepherded through the entrance turnstiles by museum staff people in lavender T-shirts with letters spelling out "Camp-In" above a picture of a dinosaur.

At last Numbles and Kevin were able to break free. They went up the escalator to the second floor of the museum's west wing, which was really more like a sort of four-sided balcony stretching around an enormous opening to the floor below. "I'm sure glad you know where you're going," Numbles said. "This place is so big it's really confusing."

"I've been here a lot," Kevin said, leading Numbles around to the left. Numbles saw that the exhibits, including the one they'd come to see, were in rooms and alcoves off the balcony. A long line of people was waiting to see the reptiles.

As they joined the line, Numbles poked Kevin. "Look at that guy," he whispered, pointing at a tall man dressed from head to toe in black. He had a gaunt face, and his eyes were hidden behind metallic sunglasses. "I wonder if he really wants to see the exhibit or if he's a high-class pickpocket."

"Pickpocket, I bet," Kevin whispered back. "There sure are a lot of weird-looking people here!"

It was true. There was a woman in orange stirrup pants and a purple tunic. A streak in her hair matched the tunic, and her lipstick matched the pants. There was an earnest-looking man in baggy olive-green cords, who kept glancing at his watch. At the edge of the crowd stood a couple of tweedy types carrying clipboards. Near them was a slender young woman with long hair as red as Numbles's. She smiled and waved red-tipped fingers at a man in sweats and running shoes who was elbowing his way toward her. "Oh, that's all right, that's all right," the man murmured to the scowling victims of his thrashing arms. "We're together; thank you."

Then Numbles stopped watching the people, because the line had moved forward. He now found himself standing in front of a huge window that looked into a room off the balcony. Behind the window—really a glass wall with a row of wooden panels about two feet high along the bottom—was a huge display tangled with vegetation, strewn about with rocks, and filled with models of prehistoric animals. A model of the ancient reptile *Dimetrodon,* its spiky "sail" rising high above its spotted back, bared its sharp teeth at a stumpy *Erythrosuchus,* while a hairy *Cynognathus* with catlike ears looked on. A pterodactyl with batlike wings hung upside down at the mouth of a cave. A painted backdrop behind what looked like a real pool showed a huge *Elasmosaurus* flexing its snakelike neck. A model of a nothosaur, like a giant newt with a tooth-lined pointed jaw, stood firmly on a rock at the shore—and a real turtle blinked up at Numbles from between the nothosaur's big clawed feet. A time line on the wall outside the display showed when all these creatures had actually lived and explained that they hadn't all lived at the same time.

"Wow!" Kevin whispered excitedly. "The dinosaurs sure look real with all those trees and stuff around them!"

Numbles nodded, but he hadn't really heard; he'd been watching a small live reticulate-collared lizard (*Crotaphytus reticulatus*). But suddenly his attention was caught by a splash at the edge of the pond. There was a gasp from the crowd as a strange slender creature emerged from the water and lumbered slowly toward the glass. It had an absurdly long neck, little hornlike appendages at the top of its head, and flipperlike legs with clawed feet. A skinny tail fanned out behind it, ending in a flat paddle. From head to tail, it was about four feet long, bigger than a large dog.

The reticulate-collared lizard fled into the cave.

The woman with the matching pants and lipstick whistled.

"It—it's a living dinosaur!" the red-haired woman squealed, flapping her painted nails.

"It's not. It's some kind of lizard," said her athletic boyfriend.

"Looks like a plesiosaur," one of the tweedy men said to his companion.

"But look at the feet," said the other tweedy man. "They're more like a nothosaur's. Big, with claws."

The man in the baggy cords came silently forward from the far edge of the crowd and pressed against the glass, breathing heavily.

"Salamander," Numbles murmured to himself, thinking out loud. "But the neck's too long. No living reptile has a neck like that."

A man in a white lab coat, obviously a museum employee, came through a door at one side of the exhibit. He smiled awkwardly, cleared his throat, and said, "Good evening, ladies and gentlemen. I see our mystery guest has decided to come out of hiding. It really is quite gregarious—seems to like people."

"Garbage," Numbles said to Kevin. "Look at its eyes. That's one mad reptile—er, amphibian. Whatever."

"Yeah," Kevin said in an awestruck tone. "It *does* seem mad."

"Or unhappy." Numbles peered closer, which wasn't difficult, because the animal had come right up to the glass. Its small head bobbed on its long, thick neck, and its clawed flipperlike front feet were crossed in front of its chest, as if in prayer. Its eyes darted around from person to person in the crowd. Numbles felt a chill when they rested on him for a moment. "It's like it's asking for something," Numbles whispered.

"Dinner, probably," Kevin said. "Speaking of which . . ."

"You go," Numbles said quietly. "I'll stay here."

"No, look," said Kevin. "I've got a better idea. Why don't we both eat now? We can come back later when the crowd's thinned out."

"You go," Numbles said again, mesmerized. The creature was staring at him, almost as if asking—no, pleading with him—for what? "I want to hear the museum guy."

Kevin shrugged, but he stayed.

"The creature was found on land," the man in the lab coat was saying, "by a party of hikers in the Adirondacks. It was sleeping near a pile of bones in a rocky cave with an underground stream in it. That's why we built a cave and a pond in our exhibit. We've been trying to determine what the creature is, but so far, we haven't come up with much. It does appear, though, that it could be some kind of missing link, like the coelacanth, that fish you may remember hearing about some years back. The coelacanth was believed to have been extinct for seventy million years, but then in 1938 someone found one off the coast of South Africa. That, of course, makes us think there could be other creatures, thought to be extinct, that actually still exist. Now, folks, I'll have to ask you to move along. There's a long line behind you."

"Rats!" said Numbles.

"Dinner," said Kevin, propelling Numbles firmly away from the exhibit. "Dad gave me ten bucks. There's three restaurants in the museum," he went on, consulting a pamphlet he'd picked up at the information desk. "We ought to be able to find something to eat at one of them."

They ended up hastily devouring burgers and shakes at a fast-food place in the east wing of the same floor as the exhibit. But the unidentified creature's pleading eyes went on haunting Numbles while he ate. "I'd give anything," he said to Kevin as they made their way quickly back, "to talk to that scientist, or keeper or whatever he is, to find out more about how they found it and what they think it is."

But the man in the lab coat was nowhere in sight when they returned to the exhibit. Instead, about fifty Brownie Scouts, including Casey, had joined the crowd—which still, Numbles saw with surprise, contained a few of the same people. The Brownies pressed up against the glass, ogling the creature, which was lumbering around the exhibit. Its flipperlike legs seemed awkward as it moved about on land, but very strong. At one point it batted impatiently at one of the trees, which swayed dangerously. The animal seemed surprised, for it backed away, blinking. Then it settled down to eat fish from a green plastic bucket. "Prehistoric plastic," Kevin remarked scornfully. "Oh, wow!"

Numbles nodded absently. The creature's eyes were amazingly expressive. After it had eaten, it seemed more content—less angry, anyway, thought Numbles, and less sad. Intelligent, though . . .

The creature suddenly reared up, pulling its head back and waving its front legs. The Brownies screamed and surged away as an angry adult voice shouted, "Casey! The man said not to bang on the glass! Now stop it!"

"Oh, no!" Kevin moaned. "Let's get out of here." He tugged Numbles by the arm.

Reluctantly Numbles followed him. When he glanced back, he saw that the unidentified animal, still rearing like a bucking horse, was now beating against the glass with its front legs. The man in the lab coat came tearing back to the exhibit and kept his eyes on it anxiously while shooing the Brownies away.

Just as Kevin pulled Numbles toward the escalator,

Numbles saw one of the tweedy men he'd noticed earlier whip out a camera and turn toward the man in baggy cords, who stepped quickly behind a nearby display case. The woman with the orange lipstick and pants shrugged into a black and white striped coat, as if to leave, but the red-haired, red-fingernailed woman stood still, staring at the upright creature from across the balcony, a faint smile on her painted lips. Funny, thought Numbles, that they all hung around so long! The man in sweats was nowhere to be seen, but the tall man in black was still near the exhibit, watching the Brownies as they were marched away. Light glinted off his sunglasses, making him look oddly like a large prehistoric insect.

GONE!

"BACK! MOVE BACK, PLEASE! No one's allowed in. Museum's closed!" a uniformed security guard was shouting to an angry crowd outside the front doors of the museum when Numbles and Kevin arrived early the next morning. A few other security guards and a great many police officers were holding people back, shaking their heads at reporters, and bustling importantly in and out of the building.

"But my sister's in there!" Kevin said, thrusting himself through the crowd; Numbles followed. "I'm supposed to pick her up!"

The security guard looked him up and down. "Name?" he asked brusquely.

"Kevin Rogoff," Kevin said. "And my sister's Casey Rogoff. Brownie Troop Number Four-eleven."

"Where are your parents?" the security guard asked suspiciously.

"Shopping. They went to New Hampshire to buy some new software and stuff. My friend Num—er, Edward—and I are supposed to pick Casey up and take her home."

"Just a minute. Wait here." The guard took a couple of steps away to where a burly policeman was standing. Numbles moved closer, but he couldn't hear what they were saying. He could hear snatches of what the people near him were saying, though, and it wasn't very reassuring: "Lost . . . No, break-in . . . One missing . . . Kidnapped, I'll wager. . . . A shame . . . Terrible for publicity!"

At last the security guard stepped back and the policeman beckoned Kevin forward. "Not you," he said to Numbles when Numbles tried to follow.

"He comes," Kevin said defiantly, "or I don't."

The policeman looked as if he was going to refuse, but after studying Numbles for a moment, he sighed and said, "Come with me." He led them through a side door into a darkish hall with more doors leading off it. Then he took them to a large office, crowded with people.

"This is the Rogoff girl's brother," the policeman said gravely to a tall bearded man in a brown suit. "Kevin, his name is. Says his parents are shopping in New Hampshire, which would explain why there's no answer at their house."

The man in the brown suit put a fatherly hand on Kevin's shoulder. "When do you think they'll be back?" he asked with a forced-looking smile.

"I'm not sure, sir," Kevin said, sounding as puzzled as Numbles felt. "But I think they're going to make a day of it. At least that's what my mom said. What—what's going on?"

"Well, son," said the man, glancing at the policeman, "I'm afraid . . . What's your first name again?"

"Kevin."

"Ah. Kevin. Fine name. And your friend?" He gestured at Numbles.

"That's Numbles. He—he's . . ."

Quickly, Numbles stuck out his hand. He knew how much his nickname confused people. "Edward Crane, Junior, sir," he said in his best talking-to-adults voice. "Numbles is just a nickname. It's a long story; my little brother couldn't say 'Edward mumbles.' But what's going on? Has something happened? Can we help?"

The man in the brown suit looked surprised, but he also looked as if he was going to let Numbles stay with Kevin, which was what Numbles wanted. "You'd both better come to my office," he said, escorting them up some stairs in what was obviously not one of the public parts of the museum.

Of course, thought Numbles. Any museum as big as this one would have to have out-of-the-way places for offices and storage and stuff. It's as if there are two museums, one inside the other, he realized as they hurried along. The private part must be just inside the outer walls, and the much bigger, public part is in the middle.

"I'm George Zave, by the way," the man in the brown suit said, coming to a stop at last and opening a door. "I do public relations." He waved them inside and pointed to a couple of armchairs as he retreated behind a massive desk and sat down. "Now then." He cleared his throat and folded his hands. "You . . . that is, your . . ." He unfolded his hands and cleared his throat again. "How old are you, Kevin?" he asked.

"Thirteen."

"And your—er—sister?"

Kevin glanced anxiously at Numbles. "Six. But what—"

"Kevin," said Mr. Zave. "There's isn't any easy way to tell you this, son. Your sister—Casey, isn't it?"

"Yes."

"Well, Casey . . . It seems, Kevin, that little Casey has—er—disappeared."

For a moment Kevin stared at Mr. Zave. Then he

smiled. And finally he laughed. "Oh, that's okay," he said. "She'll turn up. Don't worry; she's fine, I'm sure."

Mr. Zave folded and unfolded his hands again. "I—er—what do you mean?"

"She's always getting lost," Kevin explained. "Ever since she was little. She's gotten lost an average of two point one-six-six-six times a year in her life so far. I guess this time makes it—um—two point three-three-three-three. No problem. She'll turn up."

Mr. Zave looked as if he didn't know whether to be relieved or more upset than before.

"When did it happen?" Kevin asked.

"We're not sure, exactly," said Mr. Zave. "Sometime early this morning, it seems. Her Brownie leader saw her in her sleeping bag at three A.M. when she got up to take one of the other girls to the bathroom. When she got back, she thought Casey was still there because her sleeping bag was, er, lumpy. Then this morning at around six-thirty when everyone got up, Casey's bag still looked lumpy, but Casey wasn't in it. Her backpack, which the leader says she takes everywhere, was gone, too. So—"

"So," interrupted Numbles, who'd done a good deal of sleuthing with his friend Brian Larrabee, from New York, and Darcy Dixie Verona, his neighbor from Grove Hill, "so she might have gotten out of her sleeping bag even before three A.M., and—"

"And," Kevin put in, "gone exploring or gone back to see something in the museum she especially liked—dinosaurs, probably—and then gotten lost."

"The police are combing the museum now," said Mr. Zave. "But so far they haven't found any trace of her. This place is so big," he added grimly, "and has so many nooks and crannies, that looking for one small kid is . . . well, it'll take forever to search every possible hiding place. Still, I guess the police are better than we are at that kind of thing."

Kevin laughed. "Casey probably just got sleepy and curled up somewhere."

"She liked that special exhibit," Numbles said thoughtfully. "The Great Reptiles."

"Yes," Kevin agreed eagerly. "That's right. She probably thought they were dinosaurs. Just before we left, she was—well, banging on the glass."

Mr. Zave leaned forward intently.

"As if she were trying to get the attention of one of the live animals in the exhibit," Numbles said, suddenly remembering the scene vividly.

"I bet she snuck back to the exhibit after she was supposed to be asleep," Kevin said, "and got lost going back. The museum's big enough to confuse anyone, not just a kid like Casey. All we have to do is hunt for her. She knows enough to stay in one place when she's lost, and . . ."

There was a loud knock on the door. Mr. Zave called "Yes?" testily, and the burly policeman who'd been guarding the museum entrance came in.

"Excuse me, sir," he said. "Detective Barnes wants to see you. Officer Dobbin has collared a couple of suspects."

THE CRIME— OR CRIMES?

IN THE FLURRY OF ACTIVITY that followed, everyone seemed to forget Numbles and Kevin. When Mr. Zave left with the policeman, Kevin got up, too, but Numbles held him back until the two men's footsteps had faded. Then he whispered, "Come on," and they both followed cautiously, keeping well behind the men and skulking along the edge of the corridor.

The burly policeman eventually went out into the public part of the museum. He ran down a wide stairway with animal heads—wild boar, bison, and something called a Dall sheep—mounted on the bright red wall. The museum proper was crawling with important-looking men and women in business clothes, plus police and a few security guards. Numbles and Kevin followed the policeman through the east wing, past a special exhibit about volcanoes and a collection of animal statues. Then they went by the fast-food restaurant where they'd eaten the night before. A moment later they entered the west wing, where a police officer stood at each corner of the balcony.

The biggest cluster of people was at the far left-hand end, near the Great Reptiles exhibit.

Numbles was surprised to see the pants-and-lipstick woman talking excitedly to a museum security guard. He was also surprised to see police officers holding on to the red-haired woman and the man in the baggy cords. How come those people were still here, when the museum was officially closed? Had they been here the whole night? Or had they come back and somehow managed to sneak in?

"Num," Kevin said uncomfortably as they huddled behind a display case, "you don't think Casey was kidnapped or anything, do you?"

"I don't know what to think. But my friend Brian Larrabee would say to follow up every clue, no matter how strange it seems."

"Brian? The one who likes Sherlock Holmes? You're in a club with him, right? And with that girl who lives in your town, Darcy What's-Her-Name?"

Numbles grinned. "Darcy Dixie Verona," he said, knowing Darcy would far rather be called Darcy What's-

Her-Name than Darcy Dixie. "I guess you could call it a club, but it really isn't. We're pretty good at solving mysteries, though. And this looks like it's beginning to be one." He didn't think it was necessary to add that all the mysteries they'd solved so far involved supernatural creatures that most people called monsters. "You don't have suspects," he said, "unless there's been a crime. And I guess that woman with the red hair and the guy wearing the cords are the suspects the cop told Mr. Zave about. And Casey *is* missing."

"Okay," Kevin said, obviously uneasy. "But I still think Casey's probably hiding somewhere. You're the detective; you check out the suspects. I'm going to do some more looking. How about we meet back here in an hour?"

"Sure," Numbles said.

They walked to the escalator, keeping close to the balcony walls and ducking into alcoves when necessary. Then Kevin darted down the escalator, and Numbles continued on toward the cluster of people, who seemed far too intent on what they were doing to pay him any attention. There were two distinct groups, one near the reptile exhibit, and the other near an emergency exit door that was tucked away in a corner and seemed to lead to a stairwell. That group, which included Mr. Zave, had gathered into a tight knot around the red-haired woman and the man in cords, both of whom were protesting loudly.

"I told you," the red-haired woman was shouting. "I'm a reporter."

"And I'm a scientist," the man said angrily. "I'm a cryptobiologist, here to study the exhibit."

The pants-and-lipstick woman, who Numbles now saw was also part of the group, poked one of the security guards and laughed.

"And I told you," a tired-looking policewoman said through her teeth to the redhead, "that reporters have press cards." She turned to the man. "Crypto-schmipto," she said. "Sounds like hocus-pocus to me. Come with me, both of you."

"I'm free-lance," the woman said. "I don't have a press card because I don't work for any one paper. Besides, I mostly do magazine pieces."

"Cryptobiology," the man said, "is a . . ."

"Yeah, sure," said the policewoman. "And you both always sneak into museums when they're closed and when there are three hundred kids inside."

"I'm doing a story about scouting," the woman said. "Come on, I really am. If you don't believe me, you can look at my notes. Just let me get at my purse."

"We've looked in your purse, honey," the policewoman said, "and there's nothing in there resembling notes. Come on. You and your pal here have a lot of explaining to do."

"He's not my pal," the woman said angrily as a security guard opened the emergency exit door. The policewoman led the redhead down the stairs, closely followed by another officer with the man in cords, who kept saying, "You'd better let me call my lawyer," over and over.

So that's that, thought Numbles. Except if they've really kidnapped Casey, where is she?

When the suspects and the police officers escorting them were gone, Numbles waited till the guards had their backs turned. Then he ducked into the stairwell, grabbed the door as it was closing, and held it open just enough so he could hear what Mr. Zave and the others were saying.

"What do you think, detective?"

That was Mr. Zave. And Numbles figured that the detective he was addressing must be Detective Barnes, the man who the burly policeman had said wanted to see him.

There was a loud sigh, and Numbles imagined the person who made it shaking his head. "I think this museum's too big for its own good," a deep voice—the detective's, Numbles was sure—said. "I have to admit to being baffled at first. I'm confident my men have done a good job combing the place, and there's no sign of either the animal or the child. I have to ask that you keep the public out, though, until we've come up with some clues."

The animal? What animal? Numbles opened the door a crack more.

"Your chief said we could go ahead with the Omni show tonight—you know, the film in our big theater," Mr. Zave was saying. "And by the way, that 'animal,' as you call it, is a very valuable specimen—one of a kind. Several expert herpetologists and paleontologists are coming to see it on Tuesday, after the holiday. It could be some kind of missing link, I'm told, between prehistoric animals and present-day ones—very, very valuable."

"Wow," Numbles murmured to himself. "Someone must've stolen the unidentified reptile!"

"Hmm," said the detective, sounding interested. "Any rivalry there?"

"Among the scientists?" asked Mr. Zave. He sounded surprised. "I hadn't thought of that, but . . . yes, I suppose there could be. Omigosh," he said suddenly. "You don't think . . ."

"That one of those experts might want to keep the others from studying the creature? If it's as rare and important as you say it is, it seems to me that's very possible."

"You mean," said Mr. Zave slowly, "that one of the

scientists might have stolen the animal to study it or to keep the others from studying it?"

"That's exactly what I mean. Or hired a professional thief to steal it, which I think is far more likely. In fact, I'm pretty sure that the animal is no longer in the museum. Now let's go back to your office and go over the whole thing in more detail. To start with, you can give me the names of the scientists you expect here on Tuesday. I wouldn't be surprised if at least one of them knows those two suspects we picked up, maybe even hired them to do their dirty work for them."

"But what about the little girl?" Numbles heard Mr. Zave ask.

"I hate to say this," the detective answered, "but—" there was a pause, and the detective's voice got louder, as if he'd stopped and turned—"if the child witnessed the break-in . . ."

"Oh, no!" exclaimed Mr. Zave, and then both men's voices began to fade. "Her brother and his friend said she was interested in the exhibit. I suppose she . . ."

Numbles heard no more. He stayed hidden for what seemed like hours, till the voices and the bustle outside faded and stopped. Then, slowly and carefully, he crept out of the stairwell and around the corner to the Great Reptiles exhibit.

At first, it looked the same as it had before, except for

the yellow plastic tape strung in front of it, with "POLICE LINE—DO NOT CROSS" printed on it. The glass was intact; he'd half expected it to be broken. The reptile models were still there, and the live reticulate-collared lizard was perched on a rock, peering around nervously.

He noticed, though, that the pterodactyl at the entrance to the cave was tipped slightly to one side, as if someone had bumped into it. Several leaves had been stripped from a nearby tree, and the foliage behind it looked wet. And under the glass window, where the two-foot-high wooden panels stretched the length of the exhibit, was an opening. One panel was lying flat on the floor. It had apparently been removed by force, since one edge was splintered.

There was a little pile of loose dirt inside the display, near where the panel had been removed.

The unidentified animal was nowhere in sight.

A MONSTER HUNTERS JOB

CAUTIOUSLY, NUMBLES APPROACHED THE OPENING. He took a quick look around, and when he saw no one, he dropped to his knees and squeezed through.

It was weird, being inside a prehistoric scene, among prehistoric creatures—right next to a *Dimetrodon* in fact!

Numbles tipped his head up, studying the spiky "sail" growing out of the model's back. It looked so real he thought for a moment the *Dimetrodon* might be a real one, stuffed. But of course that wouldn't be possible—a prehistoric animal's skin wouldn't have lasted into modern times.

As he stood up, Numbles put his hand on the *Dimetrodon* for balance, and noticed a scratch on its side—its *plaster* side, he realized, disappointed. At least they could have used something that was more like real hide.

Numbles fingered a frond from a palm tree to his left. That, at least, was real, as were the low tropical-looking bushes and flowering plants set in sandy soil around the tree trunk. To Numbles's right was a stony area, where the reticulate-collared lizard sat among haphazardly placed boulders. The turtle was nowhere in sight.

Overhead, vines formed a thick canopy, linking the sandy and stony sides together, but it was the scene dead ahead that was most impressive. The sandy soil stretched down to the pond, forming a small beach, strewn with rocks and punctuated with clumps of heavy, thick-bladed grass. The pond itself seemed pretty big, although now that he was inside the exhibit he could see clearly where it ended.

To the left was the mouth of the cave, a rough rock structure with bits of moss and ferns clinging to it. Numbles walked over to it and stopped under the upside-down, slightly askew pterodactyl.

Maybe, Numbles thought, whoever bumped into it went inside the cave.

He peered in. Then he stepped in.

Blast it, he thought, if only I had a flashlight!

He felt his way carefully along one rough rock wall, tapping each foot in front of him before taking a step, in case the cave floor dropped off. He was surprised to feel that the floor was as rough as the walls. Why bother, he wondered, to make it authentic if people can't see it when they look through the glass?

Because, stupid, he answered himself angrily, remembering the man in the lab coat, the unidentified animal was found in a cave! The museum people probably wanted to make its home as much like the real thing as possible.

So maybe, Numbles reasoned, the creature's hiding in here—not stolen at all. If someone did break in, maybe they just scared it back into the cave.

He walked on a few steps, then reached out to see if he could feel the opposite wall. But he felt nothing but air—and suddenly he was disoriented, lost. It's no good without a light, he realized, and shivered. The unidentified animal could be right in here watching me.

Well, he thought. Maybe. But the museum people or the cops probably looked here already.

Turning, he felt along the wall with his other hand, and made his way out again.

He blinked in the bright light of the exhibit. The surface of the pond was silvery, and the palm trees cast frondy shadows on the little beach . . .

One side of which, Numbles now saw, was considerably scuffed, as if there had been a struggle there.

He knelt at the edge of the disturbed section, trying to make sense out of the scrubbed-over dirt. There was a small crisscross pattern in two spots, one right at the edge of the water, and the other a little farther back. There was also a smooth roundish indentation, with little dots at one edge.

Numbles frowned.

The marks didn't really look like footprints.

What would Brian, with his Sherlock Holmes–type mind, make of them?

Numbles walked around some more. Brian would study the whole area, he knew, searching for anything out of the ordinary, anything that didn't fit.

"But," he said softly to the lizard, whose little beady eyes followed him wherever he went, "I don't really know what's ordinary here in the first place."

"Casey?" he called softly, deciding he might as well check the exhibit for her, even though there didn't seem to be anyone around. "Casey?"

There was no answer, and he didn't dare call louder, for fear one of the security guards would hear him. As it was, he was worried one of them might go by, patrolling, and see him.

He went back into the cave, partly to conceal himself, partly to call Casey again, and partly to think.

There was no answer to his calls, so he sat down on the rough stone floor.

Okay, he said to himself. Maybe the detective's right

that someone stole the creature and kidnapped Casey, if Casey witnessed the robbery. But maybe Casey broke into the exhibit just to see it better. Or maybe she made the animal so angry when she pounded on the glass that the animal broke out.

Oh, good grief, he thought, sitting straight up. Maybe the animal attacked her!

The animal, he remembered, had seemed quite strong, and it did have those claws on its flippers. And although it had seemed more sad than fierce at first, it had certainly seemed angry later, when Casey banged on the glass.

Slowly Numbles stood up.

Brian, he thought again. This is a job for him. For all of us—for Monster Hunters.

But an unidentified, possibly prehistoric animal isn't really a monster, he reasoned.

Or is it?

He remembered the pledge they'd all signed:

> We the undersigned, being of sound mind and body, hereby swear to keep open minds in the face of all unexplained and unsolved crimes, believing that there are ancient and monstrous creatures still in the world, capable of inflicting harm and imparting terror. And we further pledge that, as Monster Hunters, we will track down all such beings

that come to our attention, and see that Justice is done.

"Ancient and monstrous creatures"—that seemed to fit pretty well.

Anyway, he decided, standing up and walking briskly out of the cave, even if the creature isn't technically a monster, this still could be a job for us!

Ten minutes later, Numbles was down on the first floor in a phone booth near the main lobby. As he'd headed for it, he'd seen that there were still police officers and security guards in the lobby, but the booth he chose was safely out of their view. He dialed the Larrabees' number in New York, charging the call to his parents' credit card. But Brian, it turned out, was in Vermont visiting his grandparents' farm for the weekend. So he called there, and luckily Brian answered the phone.

"Hi, Brian. It's Numbles."

"Numbles!" Brian exclaimed. "But you're in Boston—aren't you?"

As simply as possible, Numbles explained.

Brian let out a long, low whistle. "Wow," he said. "What a case!"

"Yeah," said Numbles. "That's what I thought. I

mean, this creature isn't really a monster, and we can't even be sure there's any connection between the two disappearances, but—"

"But it could be a monster, and there could be a connection," said Brian, and Numbles was glad to hear the eagerness in his voice. "It sounds like a job for us, anyway. You say the detective thinks both Casey and the animal have been removed from the museum?"

"Yes," said Numbles, "maybe by professional criminals hired by jealous scientists. But I don't think they have any evidence for that. The detective said they still have to look for clues."

"Do you think those people you saw the cops take away had anything to do with it?"

Numbles paused; did he? "I—I'm not sure, Brian. They did seem weird. The man said he was some kind of biologist, but I'm not sure the police believed him. And the woman didn't have a press card, even though she said she was a reporter."

"We can't discount them, then," Brian said. "Hang on a sec. Let me get a bus schedule."

It took only a few minutes for them to establish that Brian could catch a bus that would get him to Boston at around seven. "I'll have my friend Kevin meet you," Numbles told Brian. "He'll know how to get you into the museum. It's closed, but they're going to open some theater they've got, so maybe you can get in that way. Still, you might have to sneak—"

"Don't worry," said Brian. "We're good at sneaking."

"We?"

"I'll bring Darcy, of course. You know how she gets stuff done while you and I are still trying to figure out the details."

"She's home?"

Darcy went to a boarding school in Maryland and didn't get home to Vermont very often.

"Yup. For the long weekend."

"Great!"

"So, Num, hang on and don't get caught. We'll need someone on the inside when we get there. Now, about that friend of yours. What's he look like?"

Briefly, Numbles described Kevin.

"Okay," said Brian. "We're all set, then! See you later! Keep your eyes open, okay? Anything you need?"

Numbles didn't have to think. "Food," he said. "With the museum closed, I don't think they'll be opening the restaurants. But I'm going to take a good look around as soon as I hang up. I'm starving!"

"Food it is. Anything else?"

"I don't think so."

"Okay," Brian said. "See you in a few hours."

"Right," said Numbles. "Don't forget the food," he

added, for his stomach had started rumbling as soon as he'd mentioned it. "Bye."

"Bye."

Numbles hung up, then quickly made his way back up to the west wing of the second floor to meet Kevin, as they'd planned. The hour was just about up.

"The Omni Theater's in what they call the 'free zone,' " Kevin told him. "You don't have to pay to get into that part of the museum. But you can't get into the rest of the building from there. The only way to the exhibits is through the ticket gates—the turnstiles. But at least your friends could get into the building by pretending to want to go to the movie at the Omni."

Numbles consulted the museum map in the pamphlet Kevin handed him. "There are bathrooms and phones below the theater in the free zone," he said. "Maybe I could meet Brian and Darcy down there and somehow smuggle them into this part of the museum."

"Maybe." Kevin sounded doubtful. "It's worth a try, anyway. Okay. You stay here in case anything new happens and to help your friends get in. I'll call my folks. They must be home by now, and if they are, the police have probably told them about Casey. I'll tell them we're going to look around some more for her here. They'll be so upset they'll probably say okay. I . . . well, I'm upset, too, sort of. I mean, I'm not so sure she's just hiding anymore. I . . ." Kevin's voice broke a little, and he cleared his throat. "The bus comes in at seven, right?"

"Right."

"Okay. I'll be there. Good luck."

"Same to you," Numbles said. "And, Kevin, if anyone can find her, I'm pretty sure we can. Really."

As soon as Kevin was gone, Numbles headed down the deserted hall toward a sign spelling out MUSEUM CAFÉ in blue neon letters.

CLUES

THE CAFÉ WAS SMALL, just some tables and chairs in an opening scooped out of the hall. But the only food was locked up in glass cases. Numbles had already established that the fast-food place on the second floor was closed; one could go into it and sit down, but there was no way to get into the kitchen. After eluding a security guard, he found that the same was true of the Skyline Cafeteria on the sixth floor.

"So okay," Numbles grumbled to himself from near the sixth-floor stairwell. "Okay. I'll just lose some weight, that's all." He ran down the stairs. "I'll be glad when it's gone," he told the wild boar head mounted on the landing between the third and second floors. "And," he said to the ichthyosaur fossil on the next landing, "my mother will be pleased, and my gym teacher will stop making cracks at me. And maybe," he remarked to the moose head that stared at him from the landing between the first floor and the basement, "I'll even be able to . . ."

He stopped muttering and quickly flattened himself against the stairwell wall. He'd heard footsteps approaching and there was no other place to hide.

Numbles heard a sharp intake of breath down the hall, followed by a thud and a clank, as if someone had dropped something metallic, and a couple of soft swearwords. Then the footsteps went away.

Numbles breathed again and moved cautiously away from the wall. Probably a security guard, he thought, making rounds. Then he noticed something white on the floor several yards down the hall. Surely that hadn't been there before; he walked softly to it and picked it up.

It was a scrap of paper, and scrawled on it was the unfinished word "plesio . . ."

". . . saur," Numbles finished. "Plesiosaur." He looked toward where the footsteps had gone. Why would a security guard have a piece of paper with "plesiosaur" written on it?

Maybe he would, he thought, if I'm right that that's what the missing animal is related to—but why would he write it down and then tear the paper up?

Numbles heard footsteps again, so he ducked back into the stairwell. He held his breath as he heard the footsteps pass. A moment later he heard an elevator door open and close. Gears ground and machinery whirred. Numbles darted out of the stairwell just in time to see the indicator light over the elevator flash 4, 5, 6—and stop.

Numbles dashed up the stairs again and, panting, burst out onto the sixth floor opposite the Skyline Cafeteria. A man was sitting at a table there, silhouetted against the huge windows.

The man turned and looked straight at Numbles.

"Sheesh," Darcy said, heaving her backpack onto the bus's overhead rack. "I thought Mom would go on asking me questions forever and make me miss the bus!"

"Yeah," said Brian. "You should've heard my grandparents." He pushed back his unruly black hair and grinned. "But it's good to be on the job again."

Darcy grinned back. "Sure is," she said. "Even if it's not quite a monster we're after. Hey, Bri, maybe we'll branch out, huh? Into regular detective work. They're always asking in school what we want to do with our lives when we're adults. I've been saying 'detective' for a while now."

"What happened to shortstop for the Red Sox?" asked Brian, settling himself in the window seat. He glanced out, half sorry to be leaving the green hills of Vermont for the grimy streets of Boston. If he wanted grime, he could get it at home in New York. "What happened to botanist?"

"Botanist, yuck," said Darcy, sitting next to him. "That's just because of that stupid science teacher at my school who makes us collect plants. Bor-ring! Shortstop's harder to give up, but how many women have you seen in the majors lately?"

"I haven't even seen any in the minors. You picked the wrong sport, Darcy. Should've picked mine."

"Swimming's okay," said Darcy. "But you know I don't like solo sports, except running, a little. No real combat."

"Oh, come on." Brian opened the thick volume of Sherlock Holmes stories he took with him wherever he went. "The last meet I was in was pretty tough."

"You know what I mean," said Darcy. "Look, if you're going to read, at least give me the window seat, okay?"

"Sure," said Brian, and they switched.

It was lucky the elevator was still there; Numbles dashed onto it and pushed 2. When the elevator stopped, he ran out quickly, ducked into an alcove, and waited. No one seemed to have followed him. Cautiously, he peered into the stairwell. All clear.

"Okay," he said to the wild boar's unblinking stare. "Let's just check out this plesiosaur business. There ought to be a library, if this is any kind of a museum, and it ought to have reptile books if it's any kind of a library." He pulled the museum pamphlet out of his back pocket. " 'Lyman Library,' " he read triumphantly. " 'Third floor.' "

Quickly he ran up, and sure enough, the library was just to the left of the stairwell, separated from the hall by glass doors. Numbles slipped in, ran past a bee exhibit, turned right into a small reading room—and froze. Sitting at a table, with his back to Numbles, was a man in a tweed jacket, a clipboard full of papers at his side.

Tweed—the two tweedy men at the reptile exhibit!

Clipboard—that could have been what dropped.

There was a faint click, as if the library doors had opened again. Muffled footsteps headed for the reading room.

Brian closed his book and then his eyes. Evidence, he was thinking. What evidence had Numbles mentioned?

There was a lot, in a way: the broken panel, the scuffed-up dirt and the marks in it, the slightly tilted pterodactyl. There were the two suspects, too—the man in baggy cords and the red-haired woman—and of course the missing girl and the missing animal. "In solving a problem of this sort," he'd just read Sherlock Holmes remark in *A Study in Scarlet*, "the grand thing is to be able to reason backward."

That would mean backward from the crime itself.

But how could you do that when you weren't quite sure just what the crime was?

Or even if there was one?

As soon as he heard the footsteps, Numbles darted through the first open doorway he saw, which happened to lead into the library stacks, where books were stored. Flattened against a metal bookcase there, he heard the footsteps enter the reading room. Then he heard a muffled bang, as if a chair had been pushed against a table. He couldn't see without being seen, but he could hear.

"Someone else is here," a man's voice said quietly. "Somewhere in the museum."

"Probably that fanatic, Belton," said another male voice, a bit higher but just as quiet. "I bet Roderick skipped out—he scares easily. But Belton doesn't, and he's smarter. We knew he'd try something."

"I don't think it's Belton," said the first voice. "I just got a quick glimpse from the cafeteria. Looked too short, like a kid maybe."

Numbles felt his heart miss a beat or two.

There was a swishing sound—books and papers being

pushed away, probably, thought Numbles. "Maybe the missing kid," one of the men said softly.

"This kid had pants on," said the deeper-voiced man.

"Girls wear pants, Vincent."

Vincent gave a mirthless laugh. "Yeah, you're right. But he looked much too tall for a kid of six. Isn't that what they said she was? Six?"

"I think so. Maybe we should look for her."

"Oh, come on, George." The man called Vincent sounded impatient—downright heartless, in fact. "We've got more important things to worry about. You find anything?"

"Not really," George said. He sighed. "You know, Vincent, I don't think we're dealing with a known species at all."

Numbles took a cautious step closer. The two men obviously hadn't done anything to Casey, which was what he'd thought at first. They sounded more like scientists than kidnappers. Not very friendly ones, though, especially the one named Vincent.

"I mean," George went on, "we know we aren't dealing with a known species, but I don't think it's even related to anything known, not directly, anyway. The plesiosaur went on land to lay its eggs, but it was definitely a reptile—a marine reptile, not adapted to land. But this beast seems equally happy on land and in water, and it's fresh water they've got in that tank."

"That means it's evolved a lot since prehistoric times," Vincent answered. "It's adapted to fresh water and become air breathing."

I'm right, thought Numbles. They're talking about the missing animal!

There was the snap of a book being closed. "Yes," said George.

"I still think," Vincent went on, "that it's got to be related to the plesiosaur."

George gave a little chuckle. "Next thing I know you'll be telling me it's the Loch Ness monster."

Numbles blinked, trying to remember what he'd read about that. Loch Ness was in Scotland, he knew. It was a very deep lake that had once been connected to the sea. And the monster was a huge, weird-looking creature supposedly living in it. Most people believed the whole thing was just a legend, but several people claimed to have seen the monster itself. And—oh, wow, he thought, remembering a book his uncle Fred had given him—some people who'd seen it believed it might be an ancient plesiosaur that had somehow survived for millions of years!

Wow, Numbles said to himself again. I guess I really was right to call Brian!

Vincent was laughing, not pleasantly. "Sure, George," he said. "It'll be pink elephants next. Come on, let's go get some coffee. The guard isn't due to come by for a while yet, if he does at all. I've still got a full thermos downstairs, and a box of muffins."

Numbles tried not to groan at the mention of food. He waited until the men's footsteps passed back out into the entryway, and until he heard the glass doors click shut. Then he counted to five hundred, and at last went back into the reading room, scanning the tables for the book George had been reading.

But there was nothing there.

Several hours later, Brian and Darcy got off the bus in downtown Boston and looked around for someone answering Numbles's description of Kevin. "Over there," said Darcy at last, pointing to a smallish dark-haired boy walking slowly along the platform, obviously searching for someone. "How about him?"

"Kevin?" Brian called.

The boy turned, studied them for a second, and then said, "Right. Hi! You must be Brian and Darcy. Come on; the museum's still closed, but there's an Omni show we can just about make. Numbles and I worked out how he could meet you there. I sure hope you can find my sister. My parents are . . ."

"What's an Omni show?" Darcy interrupted.

"It's like a giant movie, with the screen going almost

all the way around the theater. It's neat. I guess the museum people wouldn't let the cops close the theater. People buy tickets for the Omni way in advance. Let's go; the last show's on pretty soon."

"We've got to stop and buy some food first," said Darcy. "Numbles said he hasn't been able to get any."

"Okay," Kevin agreed. "But we'd better hurry."

There were a couple of security guards in the wide lobby outside the Omni, but they didn't hinder Kevin, Darcy, and Brian from joining the crowd lined up to go into the theater. "See him?" Kevin whispered, pointing to the bored-looking guard standing near the line. "In a minute I'm going to ask him a question. When I do, you guys run down those stairs. There's rest rooms down there. If everything's gone okay, Numbles will be down there to meet you." He handed Brian a bag containing the fries, burgers, and milk shake they'd bought. "You'd better take this."

"Right," said Brian, "and you'd better take these." He handed Kevin his pack, which now had the Holmes book in it, and motioned Darcy to do the same.

"I wish I could come with you," Kevin said wistfully. "Casey's a pain sometimes, but—heck, she's okay for a little kid. She's plucky for a girl, too, but I bet she's scared. She's probably not hungry though; she's usually got food in that dinosaur pack of hers, but . . ." Kevin broke off, as if he felt embarrassed. "I just wish I could come," he said again.

Brian put a friendly hand on his shoulder. "I know," he said, "but we need someone on the outside."

"Yeah," said Darcy. "Casey may have food, but Numbles hasn't, and he can't last very long without it."

"Neither can we, Darcy," said Brian. He turned to Kevin. "How are we going to get food if they keep the museum and the restaurants closed? We might have to be here for a while."

"There are lots of lowish windows," Kevin told them, obviously trying to pull himself together. "Window frames, really, with slats over them. I guess they're vents; they've got gratings behind them. We might be able to use one of them." He paused. "I'll look on my way home. And I'll tell my folks that Numbles decided to stay with my friend Peter, that we thought that would be better because of Casey and all. But call me tomorrow—here's my number—and I'll tell you if I've found a window we can use. Of course I won't have any way of telling you how to get to it from inside the museum."

"We can look around once we get in," Brian said just as the theater doors opened.

"You'd better get going," Kevin said hastily, "before the crowd gets inside. Um—give Casey my . . . Say hi to her from me if you find her. Good luck." Briskly, he marched up to the guard.

Brian and Darcy strolled as casually as possible toward the stairs. The guard glanced their way, but as he did, Kevin tapped him on the arm and pointed in the opposite direction.

Quickly, Brian and Darcy ducked down the stairs.

Numbles felt weak from hunger—dizzy and light-headed; it was hard to concentrate. He'd spent most of the rest of the day exploring and timing the guards as they made their rounds. Luckily they didn't seem to patrol very often. There also didn't seem to be a great many of them. But maybe, Numbles thought, sitting on a bench in the little corridor under the Omni Theater, the museum's so big that the guards aren't very noticeable.

He tried to look nonchalant as people came down the stairs to use the rest rooms. Soon, though, they'd all gone back up again. A moment later Brian and Darcy came hurtling down.

"Am I glad to see you," Numbles whispered. He hustled them farther along the short corridor. "Did you bring any food?"

Brian handed him the bag.

"Thanks," Numbles said. Then with great difficulty

he added, "There's not time to eat now. First we've got to get back into the museum proper. We'll be a lot safer there. I think we'd better do it one at a time. I wish Kevin were still here to distract the guards."

"It didn't look as if there were very many guards around," said Brian, "when we came in."

"Yeah," Darcy agreed. "I saw only the two in front of the theater, plus the ticket taker. Want me to sneak upstairs and reconnoiter?"

Numbles hesitated, but Brian said, "Sure, but be careful. Darcy's so skinny no one'll even see her," he said to Numbles, winking.

Darcy stuck out her tongue at him and left.

In a few minutes she was back. "All clear," she told them. "There's only one guard up there now, and he's reading a newspaper, with his back to the stairs. The ticket taker's gone. I say we should go now—together."

Very cautiously, the three Monster Hunters crept up the stairs again, Darcy in the lead, then Numbles, then Brian. Sure enough, the only guard in sight had his back to them. Soon they had all darted away from the theater, along the hall past the Museum Café, across the lobby, and through the unsupervised turnstiles that led into the museum proper. Quickly, they dashed up to the fast-food restaurant on the second floor.

Numbles led them to a table in the back and eagerly

opened the food bag. "I've been timing the guards," he said, glancing at his watch. "I don't think there'll be one going by for another thirty minutes, if then. We'd better scrunch down anyway, though, just to be safe."

They all scrunched, and Numbles gulped down half his milk shake before starting on a burger and fries. "Umm!" he exclaimed, feeling much more cheerful. "These are the best fries I've ever had."

Darcy made a face. "Soggiest, you mean."

"When you haven't eaten for a whole day, Darcy, anything tastes good. Scientific fact."

"Fill us in," Brian said when Numbles had finished eating, and Numbles did, ending with his encounter with George and Vincent.

Brian frowned. "Do you think those guys are still in the museum?" he asked.

Numbles nodded. "I don't know quite what they're looking for, but I don't think they're going to leave till they've found it. One thing's for sure, though. They don't have Casey, since they didn't seem to know her. And I don't think they have the animal either. . . ."

"Why not?" Darcy interrupted.

They both stared at her.

"They were obviously interested in the animal," she said, "the way they were reading about plesio-whatevers and all. So maybe they have it and were trying to figure out what it is."

"I agree that they were trying to figure out what it is," Brian said slowly, "but I don't think they necessarily have the animal. 'It is a capital mistake to theorize before you have all the evidence'—Sherlock Holmes, *A Study in Scarlet.*"

"Then," said Numbles, crumpling up the empty food bag, "let's go look for evidence."

THE EVIDENCE

NUMBLES LED BRIAN AND DARCY down the hall to the west wing and the reptile exhibit.

"Clue number one," said Brian stooping over the fallen panel as soon as they got there. "There's a pretty good piece of evidence right here."

"Huh?" said Numbles.

"Has this panel been moved?" Brian asked. "I mean by the cops or the museum people after they realized the animal was gone?"

Numbles shrugged. "Looks the same as it did when I saw it earlier," he said. "But I guess it could have been moved before that."

Brian sighed and straightened up. "If I knew it hadn't been moved," he said, "I'd say it was a good sign that the missing animal got out of the display itself, instead of someone going in after it. But since we don't know whether it's been moved, we can't be sure. Let's go in."

"You mean," said Numbles excitedly, squeezing through the opening behind Brian and Darcy, "that the creature might have gotten out—escaped—instead of being stolen?"

"Right, Watson," said Brian as the reticulate-collared lizard scurried under a rock. The turtle, which had been under the *Erythrosuchus,* popped its head and limbs into its shell. *"If* the panel hasn't been touched. From the way it's lying, it looks as if it was pushed out from inside the exhibit. Of course, it'd be kind of hard for the animal to hide in the museum. Still, we've been able to—"

"Hey," said Darcy, who'd been walking around the reptile models, examining them, "all of these creepy things are nice and clean and new looking, except this baby." She patted the *Dimetrodon,* then pointed to the scratch in its side.

"Yes," said Numbles, "I noticed that, too. But there's no way to tell how long it's been there."

Brian whipped a large magnifying glass out of his pocket. "Birthday present," he announced, waving it over his head. Then he bent closer to the scratch, peering at it through the glass. "There's no dust on it," he said, straightening up. "But there is a little powdery stuff—

plaster dust, I think, probably from when the scratch was made. If that happened a long time ago, the plaster dust would be gone, and there'd be regular dust in the scratch instead."

"Except," said Darcy smugly, "I don't think a whole lot of dust could get into this display. At least not until that panel was busted."

"You'd be right," Brian said, "if it weren't for the fact that someone's got to get in here to feed the lizard and the turtle—and the missing animal. That would let regular dust in. Besides," he added, looking down at the ground, "this animal—what is it, Num?"

"A *Dimetrodon,*" Numbles replied promptly.

"The *Dimetrodon,*" said Brian, "is pretty close to all this mess." He pointed to the crisscross pattern and the dotted indentation in the sand, which Numbles had noticed earlier—plus a few new, rounded ones.

"Sorry," said Numbles, feeling his face turn red. "I guess those are my footprints." He pointed to the new marks.

"It's okay," said Brian. "Let's just be careful not to add more, okay?"

"Looks like there was some kind of fight here, huh, Bri?" said Darcy, studying the marks intently.

"Sure does." Brian raised his head. "What kind of feet does the missing reptile have, Num?"

"Big," said Numbles promptly. "Flipperlike, but with claws."

Brian frowned. "If you put your weight on a flipper," he said, "and if your flipper had claws, it might make a mark very much like this." He pointed to the indentation with the dots around it. "And this crisscross mark," he went on, "could be part of the pattern on the sole of a running shoe. A small shoe," he added, straightening up. "Did you notice what the missing kid was wearing on her feet?" he asked Numbles.

Numbles concentrated, trying to remember. Some kind of sneakers, he was pretty sure. "She could have been wearing running shoes," he said cautiously.

"Okay," said Brian. "We've got a question for Kevin, then. If Casey was wearing running shoes . . ."

"We'll know that she's been in here!" Numbles finished. "Or that she probably has. But that could mean," he added soberly, "that the animal's got her."

"We can't be sure of that part," Brian said, but his expression was grim nonetheless. "And we can't really even be sure this is her footprint unless we can get hold of a shoe of the brand she wears and see if the pattern matches. But we can be sort of sure it's hers if we find out she was wearing running shoes." He looked up at them, and Numbles could see how worried he was. "We'd better call Kevin," he told them quietly.

"Yeah, but what if his parents answer?" Darcy asked.

"Kevin's got a phone in his room," Numbles said.

Brian had been studying the marks more closely. "I think we should look around some more," he said, "before we call Kevin. You show us the rest of the evidence, Num, and then we'll call. Okay?"

Numbles agreed.

There wasn't much left to show them, really, mostly just the tilted pterodactyl, and of course Numbles couldn't really demonstrate conclusively that it had been moved. "But," he told them, "I'm sure it was more to the front when I first saw it."

"How tall is Casey?" asked Brian.

"Maybe three feet," said Numbles.

"And the animal?"

"On all fours, not as tall. But standing on its back legs and rearing up the way it did when Casey banged on the glass, maybe it was three and a half or four feet."

"That's just about the height of the cave entrance," said Brian thoughtfully. "Okay. Now I think we'd better call. It doesn't look very good for Casey, but we don't want to jump to conclusions. Remember that Holmes says to get all the evidence first."

"Sportech Panthers," said Kevin promptly when Numbles phoned him from the lobby and asked him about his sister's shoes. "I know, because I wear Sportech Leopards. They're almost the same, except for the Panthers being narrower and different colors. You mean you actually saw her footprints?" he asked excitedly.

"Maybe," Numbles said cautiously. "But don't get your hopes up. What's the pattern on the sole?" He nodded at Brian and Darcy, who were keeping watch for guards.

"Crisscrosses, I think. I'm pretty sure it's the same on Panthers as it is on Leopards."

"Wow," said Numbles. "Thanks, Kev. You just gave us a great clue. Or confirmed one, anyway."

"I hope so," he said, "because my mom's been crying all day and my dad's spent the afternoon combing the neighborhood. He thinks Casey might have run away. Num . . . the cops don't think she's just lost anymore. They told my folks they think she's—she's been kidnapped. They don't think she's in the museum. They don't think the animal's there, either. They think Casey saw someone stealing it and that whoever stole the animal took her along with it, so she wouldn't tell."

"That's possible," Numbles said quietly. "I heard a detective say that, too. But we haven't given up on her being in the museum, Brian and Darcy and I."

There was a pause.

"What do *you* think?" Kevin asked.

"I'm not sure yet, Kev," said Numbles uncomfortably, not wanting to speculate further until, as Brian said, they had all the evidence. "But we'll let you know as soon as we find anything. Okay? Got to go. Stay near your phone, though, if you can."

"Yeah, sure," Kevin said, sounding very disappointed. "I wish I could be with you guys."

"I know," Numbles said sympathetically. "But we need an outside contact, and you're it, Kev. Can you come by later with some food?"

"Yes—and that reminds me. I did find a loose grating."

"Huh?"

"I told Brian I'd look for a loose window grating to deliver food through. I found one; it's on the west side of the museum, kind of in the back."

"Great! We'll look for it around breakfast time. Okay?" Numbles said.

"Okay. Hey, good luck!"

"Thanks. Bye." Numbles hung up, turned to the others, and told them about the shoes and the possibility of breakfast.

"We'll deal with the food later," said Brian. "Never underestimate the importance of footprints," he went on grimly as they hurried back to the exhibit. " 'There is no branch of detective science which is so important and so much neglected as the art of tracing footsteps.' "

"Let me guess," said Darcy, making a face at Numbles. Then she snapped her fingers in an exaggerated way. "Got it! Sherlock Holmes."

"Brilliant deduction," Brian said dryly, and they scrambled back into the exhibit through the hole left by the broken panel.

Right afterward, two security guards came up from the emergency exit stairwell and paused outside the exhibit.

"Might as well put this panel back," one said casually, bending as if to pick it up.

Numbles, huddled with Brian and Darcy against the remaining solid part of the wood paneling, where luckily there was some thick underbrush, drew in his breath in alarm.

"Nah," said the other guard. "Better leave it. Cops said they don't want anything touched—even though they don't seem to be looking too hard anymore for that evidence they said they were after. Still, I figure we have to leave everything as is till they find the kid and the animal. I wish they'd hurry up, though, so we could fix this and open the museum again."

"Yeah," said the first guard. "You're right. I'll leave the panel where it is, just in case the cops want to look at it again."

Numbles breathed again.

"You know," the guard went on, "this whole thing is pretty fishy."

"Sure it is," said the other, chuckling. "All these reptiles. Gives me the creeps that anyone'd want to steal one. Makes my flesh crawl."

"It's not so much that," said his companion. "I mean, I can see someone wanting to steal it, if it's a missing link and all. You know scientists—always wanting to be the first to discover something. What gives me the creeps is that they took the little girl, too, when she caught them at it."

"Yeah, I know. Did you see the *Herald?* 'Child Kidnapped in Museum Plot,' it said."

The other guard laughed scornfully. "That's the *Herald* for you. At least the *Globe*'s a bit quieter—'Break-in at Science Museum.' It's more than just the little girl, though. It's this feeling I have. The kid and that confounded reptile may be gone, but it feels like the museum's full of people, you know?"

Now the first guard laughed. "You're just edgy," he said. "No wonder, with all this going on. This place can be pretty creepy at night. Come on. It's almost time for break."

Still chatting, the guards drifted away.

"Whew," said Brian as the three of them unfolded themselves and stood up. "That was close!"

"Too close," said Darcy. "I wonder how many guards there are, anyway."

She and Brian looked at Numbles. "Hey," he said, "I don't know. I'm almost as new here as you are, remember?"

Brian was already near the edge of the pond again, examining the scuffed-up dirt from one side, as if he were being careful not to add to or destroy the footprints. Numbles and Darcy went over to him and knelt; Numbles shifted a bit, because the ground was wet under his knees. . . .

The ground was wet!

"Brian," he said excitedly, "feel this." He pointed to where he was kneeling.

Brian ran his hand over the surface of the dirt, and then all the way down to the edge of the pond. Then he let out a low whistle. "This wasn't wet when we were here a little while ago," he said softly.

"It's wet over here, too," Darcy said. She had gone in the opposite direction and was standing at the mouth of the cave. "Listen!"

Numbles, followed by Brian, moved to the cave entrance.

From deep inside, he could hear a very faint scuffling.

THE MISSING MISSING LINK

"WAIT," SAID NUMBLES when Brian and Darcy started to go into the cave. "We'll need a flashlight."

It wasn't easy finding one. Numbles thought there might be some in the gift shop, but it was closed and locked. They finally found an unlocked door into what seemed to be a security guards' office. Darcy managed to snatch a flashlight off a shelf there and get back into the hall, just before a guard, with a bunch of keys jangling on his belt, came up from the floor below. All three Monster Hunters raced for a wheeled cart with what looked like aquariums on it and ducked behind it. The guard paused in front of the cart, as if he'd heard something, but then, just as Numbles thought he'd explode from holding his breath, the guard moved on.

Without speaking, the three ran back to the reptile exhibit and into the cave. If the creature did have Casey, there might not be any time to lose.

It was a little less spooky with the flashlight, but only a little. The shadows the light threw on the rough rock walls were pretty weird, bent and twisted by the rocks' jagged shapes.

"Sheesh!" exclaimed Darcy in a hoarse whisper. "It's like a real cave! Really big, too!"

"I wouldn't be surprised to find a Red Hills salamander here," said Numbles. "*Phaeognathus hubrichti,* maybe, or one of the woodland ones, the *Plethodons.* That's more likely, I guess. They're nocturnal," he explained, knowing he was jabbering out of nervousness at what they were about to find, but unable to stop himself. "And they're not entirely aquatic, like many salamanders, but they like damp places like this. . . . What was that?"

The scuffling sound—more of a rustling, really—came again and was followed by a quickly suppressed scream.

Numbles felt his heart stop. "Casey?" he called softly.

There was no answer.

"Casey?" he called again. "It's Numbles, Kevin's friend. Where are you?"

Silence again.

"Look," said Darcy. "We've got a choice here."

Numbles peered ahead as Brian aimed the flashlight to

where Darcy was pointing. Sure enough, the cave branched off in two directions. The left-hand branch seemed to go uphill, and the right-hand one went down.

"We can't just stand around deciding." Brian fished in his pocket. "Heads we go left, tails we go right."

It was heads, but there was nothing at the end of the left-hand tunnel except an open space with rock walls, floor, and ceiling.

They ran back and took the other branch.

At first it seemed to be a plain passageway, except . . .

"Shine your light around again, Bri," said Numbles, keeping his eye on one spot to his left, where the wall appeared to be somewhat rougher. "There. Stop."

He went over to the circle of light and ran his hand along the wall, up it, down it. . . .

And suddenly he nearly fell over, for his hand went into empty space.

"Whoa!" Brian pulled him to his feet. "You okay?"

"Yeah," said Numbles, "but give me the light, Bri."

Brian handed it over, and Numbles squinted into the space his arm had gone into. The edges of the hole, he saw, were really the edges of rocks, as if the hole had been made by rolling a couple of large rocks aside.

The first thing his light caught was the skeleton of a fish on the floor to one side of the opening.

Next he saw two eyes gazing mournfully into his

own—and then a smallish horned head on the end of a long neck slithered snakelike through the opening, straight at him.

"Yeoooow!" said Numbles in spite of himself, and he fell back, bumping into Brian and Darcy, who seemed to be trying to get away just as quickly as he. They all huddled against the opposite wall, staring at the creature.

But the creature just blinked, regarding them with what seemed more like curiosity than hostility.

There was no sign of Casey.

Darcy was the first to recover. "Sheesh, look at it," she whispered shakily. "I guess we've found the missing missing link."

"Yeah." Brian's voice was hushed. "I guess we have. Numbles? You're the reptile expert, and you've seen the—the thing before. Is this it?"

Numbles nodded; he still didn't trust himself to speak. Now that he was face to face with the creature, he was more sure than ever that it was not only something no one had seen before, but also something that no one had ever even imagined existed. If only he could see the rest of it . . .

Tentatively, he put out his hand, as one would to a dog, and to his surprise, the creature bobbed its head toward it, sniffing delicately, and then rubbed gently against it.

"Omigosh, Num, it likes you!" Darcy said. "It's not acting like it'd eat a kid."

Carefully, Numbles reached around and stroked the creature's head. He'd had a snake once who'd liked that, and this animal seemed to enjoy it, too, for it closed its eyes and made a low humming sound in its throat, not a purr, exactly, more like a contented song.

Then suddenly from behind the creature came a thin, high-pitched cry, saying something like, "Diney, wait!"

The animal pulled its head back and snapped its eyes open. Whipping its head back into the hole, it turned, blocking the entrance with its body.

The three Monster Hunters looked at one another.

"Casey," said Brian softly, and then he called lustily, "Casey Rogoff, are you in there?"

"Yes," came a prompt but faint reply, and Numbles almost cheered aloud. He could see that Brian and Darcy were as relieved as he. But then she said, "Don't take Diney away! Please?" and the three Monster Hunters looked at one another again, this time in amazement.

"Casey?" Darcy called uncertainly. "Who's Diney?"

"You know," came the answer. "The dinosaur. He almost left. So I tried to go, too, but he didn't want me to. He never does."

Darcy glanced at Brian and Numbles. Numbles shook his head, and Brian shrugged, raising his eyebrows. Darcy rolled her eyes at them, and then, turning back to the opening, which was now only partly blocked by the animal's body, she said, "Casey? We've come to help you. We're friends of Kevin's. You remember Numbles? He's here. I'm Darcy, and there's also Brian. We're going to try to get you out of there and take you home." Darcy glanced at Numbles as if she'd run out of things to say.

"Hi, Casey," Numbles called. "Are you okay? I mean, are you hurt or anything? Did the—the animal hurt you?"

"No, Diney didn't hurt me," Casey said indignantly. "He wouldn't. He's nice. He wants me to stay with him."

"Holy smoke," said Brian under his breath. "I guess it doesn't want to eat her—or maybe it's saving her for . . . well, for something."

Darcy made a face. "For a special treat?" she said. "Oh, gross!"

"I saw it eat fish," Numbles said slowly. "And there's a fish skeleton inside. I don't think reptiles know about treats or about saving things. I think if it was going to eat her, it would have by now. If only we were sure what it was, we could—"

"Casey," called Darcy, "has the animal eaten anything?"

"Yes," Casey said, her voice faint because the animal's

bulk was still blocking much of the entrance. But it didn't seem to mind the conversation going on through it. "He had some fish, all raw and yucky. And some green slimy stuff. He didn't want peanut butter and jelly. I've got one sandwich left in my pack, and some juice. Diney didn't want that, either."

"I don't think it wants to eat her, then," Numbles whispered to Brian.

"Casey," Brian called, "what's it like in there where you are? Is it like another cave, or what?"

"No. It's a room. A little room. Empty. Diney . . ." She hesitated a moment. "Diney likes me. He didn't like it when I banged on the glass the second time, though. I went back to visit him late at night. When I banged for him, he broke the wood and pulled me in. I was scared then, but he didn't hurt me. I think he wants to be friends, don't you, Diney?"

"Sheesh!" exclaimed Darcy, rolling her eyes again.

"Is there a door?" asked Brian, "besides the one we're at?"

"Yes," Casey said. "But it won't open. Where's Kevin? He should tell Mommy and Daddy I'm okay. They might be worried."

"Yes, honey, we know," said Darcy. "Kevin's home, and he and your mommy and daddy *are* worried. That's why we're going to try to get you out of that room, and home. Lots of people have been hunting for you." She turned to Numbles. "Can't we just shove the animal back with a stick or something, and hold it there while she gets out?"

"I don't think we'd better," Numbles said. "We don't want to make it mad."

"Maybe we could get it to come out," said Brian. "Then Casey could come out, too."

"Fish!" exclaimed Numbles. "Since it likes fish . . . Casey," he called. "Still there?"

"Of course! I'll come home later. I like Diney. He's a nice dinosaur."

"He's not a dinosaur," Numbles said automatically. Then he added, "But never mind. Look, we're going to try to get some fish for, er, Diney, and come back. If he comes out for the fish, we'll be able to get you out. Where did he get the fish he had?"

"It was already here. But he brought the slimy stuff in. Do I have to go home?"

Darcy slapped her forehead with the heel of one hand. "Yes," she said firmly. Then she added under her breath, "I guess we should be glad she's not hysterical, though."

"The slimy stuff's probably algae," Brian said. "From the pond. I bet that's why the dirt was wet; the animal went into the pond to get it. Casey," he called, "how come you didn't get out when the animal—Diney—left for the slimy stuff?"

"I didn't want to. And anyway, he put the big rocks back. He always puts them back when he goes away."

"The creature must have moved those same rocks to break into the room in the first place," Numbles said. "This reptile is really smart!"

"But it *is* holding Casey prisoner," said Brian. "It's nice that it hasn't hurt her and that she's not scared, but that doesn't change the fact that it seems to want to keep her for some reason. We'd better figure out what that reason is before we try to spring her. Let's mark the entrance," he went on, making a small pile of loose pebbles, "in case it's shut when we come back with the fish. Casey," he called, "you sit tight. We're going to get the fish now. We'll come back as soon as we can. Okay?"

Casey answered " 'Kay," unenthusiastically, and the three Monster Hunters scrambled back up the hilly passage.

"Okay," said Brian as they sat down at the mouth of the cave so they could dash back in if the guards came by. "I'm going to try to figure out where that room is in relation to the rest of the museum—the part outside the reptile exhibit, I mean—and then see if there's another entrance to it. It'd be a lot easier to remove Casey that way than through the cave."

"I hate to say it," said Darcy, "but shouldn't we tell Kevin and his folks that Casey's okay?"

"Then we'll have all the museum people in there dragging her out and doing who knows what to the animal," said Numbles. "It might turn on Casey if it felt threatened. I know she likes it and it hasn't hurt her, but we don't really know how it would act under pressure. As you said, Brian, it does seem to be holding her prisoner."

"I wish," said Brian, "that we knew what it was. Do you have any idea, Num? Why do you think it's got her?"

Numbles shook his head. "I don't know any more than I've already told you about what it might be. If it's a plesiosaur . . . well, I don't know much about them. And I don't know why it's got her, especially since it doesn't seem to want to eat her, and since it was so gentle with me. Maybe it's lonely. She sort of said that."

"Oh, come on, Numbles," said Darcy. "It's only a reptile! *He's* only a reptile," she corrected herself. "At least Casey seems to think it's a boy."

"Since when are you an expert on reptiles, Darcy Dixie Verona?" Numbles snapped back.

Brian stood up. "Come on, guys, we've got too much to do to fight. Why don't you two look for some fish?

And something for Casey to eat, too. She said she's only got one sandwich and some juice left. Just try not to swipe any rare exhibits," he called after them.

Darcy said she'd take the lower floors, so Numbles went upstairs, deciding to start with the sixth floor; maybe he could find a way into the cafeteria kitchen.

The doors to the kitchen wouldn't budge, and he found nothing but a few packages of sugar out on the counters. The other doors on that floor were locked, and so were the doors leading off the stairs to the fifth and fourth floors, so he ended up back on the third floor, where the library was. He hadn't checked out the exhibit next to the library, so he poked his head into that. It was a strobe light exhibit, not a fish one. He went out into the hall again and was wondering where to look next when he felt a strong hand seize his shoulder from behind. Another hand clapped itself over his mouth before he could even think about yelling for help.

CAPTURED!

THE NEXT THING NUMBLES KNEW, someone had slipped a gag over his mouth and a blindfold over his eyes. Someone else—or maybe it was the same person—was pulling, dragging, and pushing him forward. No one said anything, and it was weird, like being in one of those dreams in which you want to run but can't, because your feet are like lead and your legs feel like clumsy bags of straw. Numbles knew it would be useless to yell, since the only sound he could make through the gag was a muffled squeak.

"Stairs," an oddly familiar male voice said sharply, and instantly Numbles felt himself plunge downward. After a couple of false starts, his feet somehow gauged the height of the steps, but he almost fell when the stairs stopped and then started again. Okay, he said to himself, that must have been a landing, and landings usually come halfway down a flight, so even though we've gone down two sets of stairs, it's probably only been one floor, so we must be on the second floor now. . . .

Another flight of stairs. Another landing. More stairs. Then more again, another whole set.

So this must be the basement, Numbles reasoned.

He heard a few clicks and a whoosh—a heavy door being opened? Then he felt cold air on his face. Oh, no, he thought, near panic; they're taking me out of the museum! Unpleasant visions of people being "taken for a ride" in cop shows on TV rose in his head. It didn't help that the ground underfoot was hard, like pavement.

The pavement sloped sharply down—a hill, Numbles told himself, thinking it might be useful to remember the terrain—and then leveled off . . .

Suddenly Numbles was shoved down to a sitting position—So I can't be in a car trunk, he thought—and then someone ripped the blindfold off and removed the gag as well.

Numbles blinked and looked around.

He wasn't outdoors at all, but in what seemed to be a basement corridor. Near one end was a window protected by a heavy grating, but there was no visible outside door, although there was a heavy-looking interior one.

Standing over him, staring down at him severely, were the two tweedy men.

Numbles blinked in surprise.

"Where's Belton?" one of them demanded. He sounded like George, one of the men Numbles had overheard in the library. He had a long, skinny neck—like a giraffe in a sport coat, Numbles thought, choking down a nervous laugh.

"Huh?" Numbles said stupidly.

The other man was round and ruddy compared to George. He reached down and shook Numbles's shoulder roughly. "You heard my friend," he snarled, and Numbles instantly recognized Vincent's voice. "Where's Belton? Or Dr. Belton, as he probably calls himself to you. What are you, his kid or something? Hmm?" He shook Numbles again. "Come on," he said. "Speak up!"

"Wait." George put a restraining hand on Vincent's arm. "Maybe the kid's with Roderick. Remember Roderick said something about maybe hiring a young assistant." He gave Numbles a forced-looking smile. "Is that it?" he asked. "Are you interested in taxidermy? Did Mr. Roderick hire you?"

"I—I don't know what you're talking about," Numbles managed to say, adding "I'm terribly sorry" for good measure, since that usually impressed adults. Taxidermy, he thought. That's stuffing dead animals, like those stuffed squirrels and wolves and foxes in natural history museums.

The two men looked at each other. Then George knelt down in front of Numbles. "Look, son," he said, almost kindly, "we're sorry we brought you down here like this, but we know you've been skulking around the museum, and the museum's closed. Mr. Roderick works for us, but he's disappeared, and we're not sure why. We think that he or Dr. Belton—who doesn't work for us—has stolen the—er—the supposedly unidentified animal from the Great Reptiles exhibit. Now, as you can imagine, that's a very bad thing to have done, and it's very important that the animal be returned so it can be studied and classified, and so . . ."

"George," Vincent said impatiently, "he's a kid. What does he care about all that?"

"Oh, no," Numbles told them eagerly. "I *do* care, I care very much. I'm—er—you see, I'm president of the Herpetology Society at home in Vermont." He held out his hand. If these guys are scientists, he thought, and if they're worried about the animal's being missing, they must be all right even if they do have a taxidermist working for them. "Edward Crane, Junior," he said with what he hoped was an ingenuous smile. "My friends call me Numbles."

Vincent groaned angrily and turned away, but George

smiled and shook Numbles's hand. "How do you do?" he said. "George Feeney here. And that's my colleague, Vincent Butterworth. We're paleontologists, actually, but we have great respect for herpetology. After all, a lot of what we study is reptiles."

"Oh, stuff it, George," Vincent snapped. "The kid probably doesn't even know what a paleontologist is."

"Yes, I do," said Numbles politely. "A paleontologist studies prehistoric animals—studies fossils, puts dinosaur bones together—ancient reptile bones, too." He hesitated a moment, then asked, "What do you think the unidentified animal is? If you don't mind my asking? I mean, it looks kind of like a plesiosaur, don't you think? But then there are those feet, more like a nothosaur's, and some of it doesn't look much like anything known, or at least anything I've heard of, but . . ." Numbles stopped. The two men were staring at him, especially Vincent, the really nasty one. Had he said too much? Had he given away the fact that he'd seen the creature up close?

But shouldn't he tell them where it was, that it hadn't been stolen at all?

George bent closer to him. "If you know that much, kid, you'll know that if we're going to identify this creature, we've got to get a good look at its bone structure, its skull in particular, to see if it's euryapsid or diapsid, for one thing, and—"

Vincent interrupted. "We're wasting time, George," he said impatiently "The kid may know his snakes and frogs, but he's not going to know euryapsid from diapsid, and we've got to—"

"An animal with a euryapsid skull pattern," Numbles said calmly, but a little proudly, too, "has a pair of holes in the upper part of its skull. That shows it lived in the ocean—was a marine animal of some kind, like a plesiosaur. As far as anyone knows, there aren't any reptiles anymore with that skull pattern. But lots of living reptiles—snakes and lizards and crocodiles—have a diapsid pattern, two or more pairs of skull holes. Wow," he added, impressed. "I can see why you'd want to know that!"

"Yeah," said Vincent darkly, "but we're never going to find it out if that creep Belton gets his mitts on the animal. Listen, kid, he's not interested in scientific research. Belton's trying to get all the glory for himself, without doing any of the work. He's just interested in the animal as a—as a curiosity."

"You mean," said Numbles slowly, his brain reeling, "the way a circus person would be?"

The two men exchanged a glance, and then Vincent grinned unpleasantly. "Yeah," he said. "You might say that. Yeah."

Something in his tone, though, put Numbles on

guard. Taxidermy, he thought again. Wait a minute. If these guys really want to study the animal's skull patterns . . .

He gulped inwardly. How could they study skull patterns, he thought, without seeing the skull itself?

At best that would mean X-rays or surgery, and how would anyone be able to predict if a rare or unknown animal would survive that? And at worst, if they were working with a taxidermist . . .

Numbles shuddered. "I wish I could help you," he said craftily. "But I really don't know who Dr. Belton is, or Mr. Roderick, either, and I'm really not working for anyone."

"I think he's telling the truth, Vincent," said George, pulling his friend aside and talking in a low voice, but not so low that Numbles couldn't hear.

"I'm not so sure," Vincent said. "What do you say we leave him here awhile just to let him think things over? Let him get a little hungry, a little thirsty . . ."

"Is that really necessary?"

"Do you want this find or don't you?"

"Yes, of course I do," said George.

"Well, then . . ."

"Okay, okay. But not too long. Kids have parents; we don't want to get into trouble about this."

"It's a risk we've got to take. George, this is the find

of the century, you know that! If this animal is what we think it is—"

"I know, I know." George sighed. "If it's what we think it is, we'll be very rich and very famous. Okay. But no more rough stuff. Promise?"

"I promise."

The two men walked back to Numbles.

Rich and famous, Numbles was thinking. Is that all they care about? Even George? What about the animal itself?

"Ed," Vincent began in an exaggeratedly pleasant voice.

"Numbles," George corrected.

"Right—Numbles." Vincent knelt down so he was at eye level with Numbles, but he kept his face a respectful distance away this time. "Maybe you're telling us the truth. But maybe you aren't. You've got to admit you know a lot for a kid. And you've got to admit that we've got a lot at stake here. If you're on the level, I know you'll agree it's important that we find this animal, and so you'll understand why we have to be careful. We're still not convinced you don't know Belton. So we're going to let you think it over. We'll come back in a while to see what you've decided. Okay?"

No, Numbles wanted to say, it's not okay! I've got to warn Brian and Darcy, and we've got to do something to protect the animal from you, since I bet you're going to crack its skull open just so you can have the glory of finding out what it is, and then you'll have your friend Roderick stuff it so you can make a lot of money selling it to a museum!

But aloud he said meekly, "Okay. I don't like it a lot, but okay."

"Good man," said George. "I'm sorry we have to do this, but I guess you do understand. After all, you *are* president of the Herpetology Society, right?"

"Yeah," said Numbles. "Right." And that, he thought, is why I'm not going to tell you guys anything—because a rare specimen ought to be protected—alive!

"See you later, then," said George, and he and Vincent went quickly up the incline to the heavy-looking door at the far end. It swung shut with a loud click when they went out.

Numbles figured there wasn't much point in his trying the door, but he did anyway, a few minutes after the two men left.

It was tightly locked.

He walked to the opposite end of the narrow corridor—gray concrete walls, ceiling, and floor—and examined the window grating. It was just low enough for him to reach about halfway up it, and it was a little loose, but like the door, it was locked. He could see a padlock dangling from the bar that closed it, but that was too high for him to reach, and though he tried, Numbles wasn't able to pull himself up to it. "Darcy could, I bet," he grumbled. "Brian, too. I guess it pays to be an athlete." But, he realized, even if they could pull themselves up to the lock, without a key or a hacksaw they'd be unable to do anything further. And anyway, on the other side of the grating there seemed to be wooden slats, probably for ventilation, he decided.

Discouraged, Numbles turned away—and saw what seemed to be a crack near the base of the wall.

He stooped to examine it, and saw instantly that it wasn't a crack at all. It was the outline of a small door, flush with the wall and the same color. The crack was pencil-thin, and the door fit very tightly, which was why he hadn't noticed it right away.

It also had an almost invisible handle that folded flat into a little indentation, and when he lifted it up, the door pushed in easily. There was a latch on the inside, so, he reasoned, it could probably be locked from there.

It was dark inside, but when his eyes grew accustomed to the lack of light, Numbles could see a passageway the same height and width as the door itself—about two feet square.

Cautiously, taking a deep breath and holding it to make himself as small as possible, he squeezed inside.

Just a few feet in, he came to what seemed to be another wall, only this one was metal, with tiny holes in it, and a thin, fuzzy coating that came away when he pulled at it.

In the dim light from the corridor, he could just make out the words in the upper left-hand corner:

HC Plumbing and Heating
Air-Conditioning and Heating Units
Residential and Commercial
For repairs call 617-555-4811
For best results, clean filter monthly

So it was just a heating or air-conditioning duct, with a filter.

Disappointed, Numbles crawled back out and closed the door behind him.

Now what?

There wasn't anything left to explore, so he sat down again, leaning up against the wall.

George and Vincent are paleontologists, he thought, which must be why they were in the library, looking things up. But they sure are greedy! They obviously want to get the jump on those other scientists who are supposed to arrive on Tuesday. I bet they'd have stolen the animal themselves if they'd had a chance. They can't be very ethical scientists if they want to destroy a specimen just so they can make money from it.

But what about that other guy, Belton? If he's a circus person, he's just as bad. He'd probably put the animal in a cage and truck it around for people to gawk at. The animal might be better off dead!

Numbles remembered the pleading look in the animal's eyes, the way it had responded to his stroking, and how intelligent it had seemed. Poor thing, he thought. It probably wishes it were back at home, wherever home is. . . .

He sat up straighter. Wait a minute! What did that guy in the lab coat say when he came out to explain about the animal? Something about the Adirondacks—a cave with bones in it? Wait . . . There was something else, too. . . .

Numbles got up and began pacing.

Adirondacks—cave, he thought. Cave. Adirondacks—that's New York State, not far from Lake Champlain. Omigosh!

Numbles froze, stunned. Of course! Why hadn't he thought of it before? George had even mentioned it himself, although he hadn't seemed serious about it. Loch Ness monster, he'd said.

Lake Champlain had a monster, too; Numbles had read about it in the book Uncle Fred had given him about the Loch Ness monster. Champ, it was called, as the Loch Ness monster was called Nessie. The two creatures were supposed to be very similar. According to some theories, they were the same kind of animal, the same kind of missing link between prehistoric and modern times.

Missing link. Hadn't the guy in the lab coat said something about that? And about an underground stream in the cave?

If so—and if the underground stream led to Lake Champlain—and if the animal looked kind of like a plesiosaur—then there was quite a lot of evidence that it was the Lake Champlain monster!

Or *a* Lake Champlain monster. Numbles remembered Uncle Fred's book mentioning a theory that there was more than one—maybe a whole breeding colony of monsters. Like Loch Ness, Lake Champlain was thought to have had an outlet to the sea in prehistoric times. People thought Loch Ness monsters, if they were plesiosaurs or something like plesiosaurs, had somehow survived into modern times and gone through mutations to enable them to live in cold fresh water instead of warm sea water and to enable them to spend at least some time on land. That's what George and Vincent had said this animal did and that's what Numbles himself had seen it doing!

If that cave in the Adirondacks was full of bones, Numbles reasoned, that could be the answer to Uncle Fred's main argument against the existence of the monsters. Uncle Fred always said that if the monsters were real, someone would have found the dead ones' bones. But maybe, Numbles thought triumphantly, when they're going to die, they swim down an underground stream to a cave and die there.

Or the living ones somehow take the dead ones there, like taking bodies to a cemetery.

Of course the animal here in the science museum is small, a lot smaller than Lake Champlain monsters are supposed to be.

Well, thought Numbles, maybe it's young—*he's* young, he corrected himself, remembering Casey seemed to think the monster was male. That might explain why he got caught.

He's sure the right shape and everything.

Numbles was so excited he couldn't sit still. It was awful, not having anyone to tell.

It was awful, too, that the animal—the monster—Champ—was in danger of being killed or exhibited.

We've got to get him out of here, Numbles realized. Fast!

He was just going to try the door again when it opened and George and Vincent came in.

Vincent pushed him back rudely. "Oh, no, you don't," he said. "You're staying right here."

"Have you changed your mind?" asked George, removing Vincent's hands from Numbles's shoulders.

"I—there's nothing to change," Numbles said. "I told you, I don't know Dr. Belton or Mr. Roderick. I've never even met them. I don't know what they look like."

"Roderick's skinny," said George. "He wears sunglasses, the metal ones you can't see people's eyes through. And Belton's kind of serious looking. When we saw him here he had on a pair of baggy corduroy pants—green, I think. Dingy green."

Numbles stared at him.

"Aha!" said Vincent triumphantly. "What did I tell you, George? He does know them—one of them, anyway." He moved closer to Numbles. "Maybe Belton's using another name, huh? Come on, kid, what do you know about him? How long have you been working for him? How much did he pay you to spy on us, huh?"

"N-nothing," Numbles stuttered. Vincent's face was almost touching his again, and since Vincent had backed him up against the wall, he couldn't move away. "Really. I don't know him, honest. But—but I think he's been arrested, if he was wearing baggy corduroy pants. At least

I saw the police take away a guy who—who was dressed like that. So if I'm right, your Dr. Belton's in jail."

"Not anymore," came a surprisingly calm voice from the door.

George and Vincent whirled around and then lunged forward.

The moment their backs were turned, Numbles darted to the door of the heating and air-conditioning duct, scrambled inside, and latched it behind him.

ALARM!

DARCY HAD FOUND NOTHING on the lower floor except lots of inconspicuous doors that could have led almost anyplace. But they all were tightly locked.

Discouraged, she made her way back up to the second floor. Maybe that pond's got fish in it, she thought. Maybe I could dive in, or rig up a fishing pole.

When she got to the top of the escalator, she saw a set of glass doors she hadn't noticed before. They were ahead of her and slightly to her left, and led to something called SunLab. It didn't sound very promising, but when she saw glass tanks inside, she went in.

She found herself in a short hallway, with a greenhouse to her left, plus some workbenches with odd-looking apparatus on them. Straight ahead was another set of glass doors, a great many more plants, and two or three large fish tanks, with buckets nearby. There was a sink, too, with flowerpots and empty cans and jars on a shelf above it.

There was nothing to indicate that the fish in the tanks were particularly rare or valuable, so Darcy reached down for a bucket she could use to snag one. Just as she touched it, though, someone grabbed her shoulder, and as she whirled around indignantly, a man's voice shouted, "I've got her!" In a softer voice, the man said soothingly, "It's okay. You're safe now. We'll get you back home to your mom in no time. I've just got to let everyone know . . ."

A moment later a loud alarm bell sounded throughout the museum.

There was no door, no possible entrance to the room Casey was in, Brian was sure of that. He'd walked around the reptile exhibit a hundred times if he'd done it once; he'd also studied the museum map and figured out where the room ought to be. That was a little hard, since the reptile exhibit was too new to be on the map. But he'd been able to figure it out pretty well, and there was no space for a room there that he could see.

At least not on the second floor.

Of course the cave tunnel floor had sloped *down.*

Brian consulted the map again.

The reptile exhibit was next to something called the Cahners Theater. And below the Cahners Theater, on the first floor, were . . . water exhibits!

Of course—the pond! The water for the pond had to come from someplace, and if the museum had water exhibits, then . . .

Brian rushed to the escalator and ran down it to the first floor.

Sure enough, there was a big sign saying that the Giant Wave Tank was temporarily closed, as were the other water exhibits.

But the entrance to the room, if there was one, would have to be down here, someplace off the exhibit area.

He was just about to push his way past the curtains and partitions that closed the water exhibit off from the public when an alarm bell rang throughout the museum.

It was very stuffy inside the heating and air-conditioning duct, and very cramped. Numbles wanted to rub his aching legs, but he couldn't reach them well enough to do it.

The angry voices had faded a bit, but he didn't dare check to see if anyone was still in the corridor.

His stomach had started to grumble again. It must be time for breakfast, he thought—past time, probably; he was starving. Sleepy, too. Brian and Darcy must be sleepy and hungry, too, he reasoned; we've been up all night.

What if George and Vincent find Champ? Or what if Belton does? What if that Roderick guy is lurking around here, too?

We've got to get Champ out of here, he thought.

Of course we've got to get Casey away from him first. But then we've really got to get him out of here.

Sure, Numbles, he told himself scornfully. Just run back, say, "Come on, Casey," snap a leash on Champ, and lead them both happily away. Into the sunset.

Numbles, he scolded himself, if you can't think constructively, don't think at all.

He tried to make his mind a blank, but that didn't work. It's funny how you can't do that, he thought. Even if you think about not thinking of anything, you're still thinking of something. Weird. I wonder if there's a scientific name for that, or a reason . . .

Then for a moment he did stop thinking, aware that the angry voices outside his hiding place had stopped completely.

Cautiously, painfully, Numbles eased around till he was able to reach the latch with his hand. He cracked the door open slightly and peered out.

No one.

He opened it a little more.

Still no one, so he uncurled himself and slid out.

He looked to the right and to the left—and to the left again. The corridor was empty, but there was something on the floor below the window. Something largish and brown and paper—a paper bag! Two bags—no, three! Kevin? Kevin! So it must be morning—"Breakfast time," he'd told Kevin—and the window here must be the one with the loose grating Kevin said he'd found!

His mouth already watering, Numbles ran to the bags and ripped them open. Doughnuts! Wonderful plump sugary cinnamon doughnuts! Crisp plain doughnuts! Oozing jelly doughnuts! A French cruller! Three corn muffins!

For a moment, Numbles ate happily, conscious only that his stomach welcomed the food, his head cleared and felt less dizzy, and his limbs grew stronger.

But then he put down the bag he was holding and stared at the window.

He'd missed Kevin. He'd missed the best chance he'd had to communicate with the outside, to let the others know he was trapped in this blasted corridor—but was that still true?

Numbles ran to the door at the far end of the corridor and tried to turn the knob.

Yes, it was locked.

He was still a prisoner.

Okay, he thought. Think, Numbles. Kevin said the window was in the back of the museum.

But the more he thought about it, the more he realized it wasn't a very useful piece of information. The important thing now was to figure out how to get out of the corridor and back *into* the museum, not out of it.

There didn't seem to be any way of doing that, though.

Unless . . .

Resignedly, Numbles turned back to the duct door. The idea of going back inside that tiny space made his legs ache all over again. Still, a proper duct had to lead someplace. If the filter inside it was removable . . .

It was.

And so Numbles, shoving the empty doughnut bag into his pocket and pushing the two full bags in front of him, squeezed back into the duct. He latched the door behind him, laid the filter carefully on the duct floor, and started crawling.

"BEFORE SOMETHING REALLY TERRIBLE HAPPENS"

"YOU DON'T UNDERSTAND," Darcy said desperately. "I'm not the kid you're looking for. I'm not Casey Rogoff. I'm Darcy Verona."

The policeman, whom the security guard had called, studied her skeptically, then turned to the guard who'd taken her to the security chief's office.

"You found her in the SunLab?" the chief asked.

The guard nodded.

"What are you doing in the museum if you're not Casey Rogoff?" asked the policeman, turning back to Darcy. "The museum is closed."

"Must be another Camp-In kid," said the guard. "That right?" he asked Darcy.

Darcy realized it would be a lot easier to say she was

than to say she wasn't. She could even pretend she was upset or lost—that sort of thing. Anything would be better than having to explain what she was really doing in the museum.

"That's right," she said, and with a superhuman effort she managed to make her lower lip tremble a little. "I got lost. I went away from the others, and then I couldn't get back—"

"Were you with the Rogoff kid?" asked the policeman.

"N-no, sir," Darcy told him, warming to her role. "I—I'm not even sure who she is. I—I'd just like to go home, please. I have to get my stuff, though, and—and go to the bathroom. I have to go to the bathroom real bad."

The security chief sighed. "You guys have a female officer here?" he asked.

The policeman shook his head.

"We can't very well go with her to the bathroom."

"Oh, that's okay," Darcy said. "I know where I am now. Look, I'll just go and then get my stuff, and then I'll come right back, okay?" She gave them her widest, sunniest smile. "I'm sure glad you found me," she said. "I didn't know where I was or anything." She started to leave, but the policeman stood in her way.

"Wait a minute," he said suspiciously. "What were you going to do with that bucket?"

Darcy tried to look embarrassed. She tried hard to

force herself to blush, but that didn't seem to work, so she looked down at the floor, giggled, squirmed a little, and said, "You know."

The policeman did blush, and he let her go. "Come right straight back," he called after her.

"I will," she answered, but as soon as she was away from the office, she ran as fast as she could to the reptile exhibit, only to see a tall man in tweeds squatting outside it, peering into the opening left by the broken panel.

Skidding to a stop, Darcy ducked into the exhibit next door, which was a facsimile of a rain forest, complete with a botanist's tent on one side and shrubbery dominated by a thick tree trunk on the other. There were some benches, and wooden steps led up to a small, low balcony halfway up the trunk. Vines covered the whole display, forming a greenish canopy overhead. The sounds of the museum outside were masked by bird calls and insect buzzes. The whole exhibit was dark and realistic and seemed a perfect place to hide.

Darcy scurried up the rough wooden steps to the balcony, where she found a cot and a lot more vines. She was about to squeeze under the cot when it moved slightly and a voice whispered, "Occupied. Try the tree trunk. Put that net over you."

"Brian?" Darcy whispered when her heart had recovered from the lurch it had given.

"Yes. Shh. Is that tweedy guy still at the Great Reptiles exhibit?"

"Yes." Darcy eased herself behind some fine-mesh netting that was draped around the thick tree trunk. She could just make out Brian, whose body, she saw, was serving as a platform for the cot. Because it had a set of legs in the middle, there wasn't as much room underneath it as she'd thought.

"Did you hear the alarm?"

She grinned. "That was because of me. They caught me—thought I was Casey. But I got away. Where's Num?"

"I don't know. Shh. Someone's coming."

Footsteps approached the rain forest exhibit, slowed, and entered. A quiet rustling and a muted thud told Darcy that someone had probably sat down on a bench below, opposite the botanist's campsite.

More footsteps.

More creaking.

Then voices: "Anything?"

"No. It all seems the same."

"What was the alarm?"

"I heard a guard say that they found the missing kid."

Sure they did, thought Darcy sarcastically.

"Good. Maybe they'll stop prowling around so much."

"Not likely, with the specimen still gone."

"That other kid can't get out, can he?"

Darcy gasped. What other kid? Where was Numbles?

"Not unless he's a Houdini. That door's secure."

"So now all we've got to do is find the specimen before Belton finds it."

"Or finds us again. Blast Roderick for running out on us."

"Yeah. Have you got the dart gun?"

"Yup. And the darts."

"Good."

"If there's any more human interference, I'm going to use them. Time's running out, and I think those darts will work on humans as well as on our slippery friend."

"You still think it's in the museum, right?"

"Don't you?"

"I don't know, Vincent. We sure aren't finding it, you know what I mean?"

"It's got to be somewhere, George. It's got to be somewhere."

There were a few more creaks, then footsteps moving away, and at last silence.

"Sheesh." Darcy untangled herself from the netting and joined Brian, who had slid out from under the cot and was now sitting on it. "Talk about suspects! Do you suppose they've got Numbles?"

"Sounds it, doesn't it?" said Brian.

"And it sounds like they're going to—I don't know—shoot darts into the animal." She shuddered. "Or at anyone who gets in their way."

"Yeah, it does. What we don't know is why, though. This case is more complicated than I expected. And a lot more dangerous. Come on. I think we'd better go back to Casey. Did you get any fish? Or any food for Casey?"

"No. Did you find the room?"

"No. As Monster Hunters we make pretty good . . . Oh, I don't know."

"Cheer up, Bri," Darcy said. "We did okay as Monster Hunters. We found the monster, after all. Or the whatever. It's just everything else we're no good at."

"We'd better improve pretty fast," Brian said. "We've got to figure out what to do about Numbles. I have a feeling we don't have much time before something really terrible happens."

It was hard work, crawling along the duct. The floor, or what amounted to a floor, was smooth and slippery, and there was nothing to hold on to except an occasional metal band that joined two sections of the duct together. Although there was a little room to spare on either side, there was barely enough overhead for Numbles to sit upright. He had to pull and push himself along on his belly as best he could—like a marine, he told himself, but since he didn't have much interest in being a marine, that didn't help. It was hot in there, too. Soon his face was wet with sweat and his shirt was stuck clammily to his back. Sometimes, too, the duct branched, and Numbles had to decide which way to turn. The first time, he'd tried to figure out which way to go, but since he had no idea where in the museum he'd started from and little idea of where he wanted to end up, there didn't seem to be much point in that. He turned left the first time, and then right, and then left again . . .

Suddenly the duct ended. At least something blocked his way. Another filter, he thought, pulling at it.

Sure enough, it popped out—and left him facing a glass wall, behind which he could clearly see water.

Swimming in the water was none other than Champ himself.

REUNITED

IT HAD TO BE; there was no longer any doubt in Numbles's mind about the identity of the creature he was facing.

For a moment he forgot where he was and just studied Champ. The monster was rather beautiful underwater, dolphinlike, swimming and turning gracefully, using his tail as a combination rudder and paddle and his legs as additional paddles. His horned head, on the end of a long neck, seemed to be scouting in front of him, although once in a while it would turn upward and disappear, as if searching the surface for food or air. His body and tail were flexible enough to bend into the humps many people had sworn they'd seen at Loch Ness or Lake Champlain. Of course this monster was smaller than those

Numbles had read about, but that would be true if he were young, Numbles thought again. This animal's tail and legs were a little different from those usually described, but since no one had been able to photograph a Champ or a Nessie really close up, no one could really be sure what a lake monster's legs and tail looked like anyway.

More than ever Numbles knew he had to find a way to return Champ to the lake, where he belonged.

Casey, too, of course, he added hastily, suddenly realizing that Champ must have left her alone again.

But he would probably have put the rocks back over the entrance to keep her in.

Champ did a sharp flip with his tail, bringing his face up close to the glass. Blinking, he surveyed Numbles while he backwatered with his flippers and tail, holding his body in one position.

Numbles returned his stare. Champ certainly didn't look fierce, even though he was holding Casey captive. Numbles could see why she liked him.

Champ turned away silently, so Numbles tapped gently on the glass.

Instantly Champ turned back, with his mouth in an almost-smile, and brushed one flipper against the glass. Numbles tapped again and kept his hand on the glass; Champ put his flipper on the other side, where it would have been against Numbles's hand if there hadn't been any glass there. He gazed at Numbles sadly.

"We'll get you out," Numbles whispered. "I promise. At least we'll try. We'll get you out and home again, away from all those fake scientists. Only you've got to give up Casey, the little girl. . . ."

Dope, he said to himself. You'd think he could hear you! Even if he could, he couldn't possibly understand.

Numbles turned away and, pushing the bags of doughnuts ahead of him again, he crawled back to the last intersection in the tunnel, his mind still on Champ. I wonder, he thought, who kidnapped him. . . .

Kidnapped!

Numbles stopped crawling. Could that be it? Since Champ had been kidnapped and probably wanted to go home, could he have kidnapped Casey to hold her hostage until he was returned to his home?

It seemed farfetched—too human. What was that word for when you gave animals human characteristics? Anthropomor-something? Anthropomorphism.

But if they couldn't get Casey away from Champ, maybe he and Brian and Darcy could somehow take both Champ and Casey to Lake Champlain and see if Champ would free Casey once he was home.

Sure, Num, he said disgustedly, deciding to take the other fork in the tunnel this time. Sure, take Champ to

Lake Champlain. How? On the bus? Right. Numbles almost laughed out loud at the spectacle of their trying to buy a ticket, let alone save a seat, for a Lake Champlain monster!

If we were only old enough to drive . . .

Numbles stopped again.

Uncle Fred can drive, he said to himself, and then a plan slowly began to form in his mind.

This time it was security guards who came by and almost caught Darcy and Brian, who were sitting on the rain forest balcony cot. Brian barely had time to get the cot on top of himself again, and Darcy just managed to dive behind the netting before two guards paused just outside the exhibit.

"Fishy, still," one of the guards was saying.

"Oh, come on, Max. We've both done complete rounds twice and we haven't found anything." He peered into the botanist's tent, then climbed halfway up the balcony steps and glanced at the tree trunk and the cot. Darcy crossed her fingers until he went down the steps again.

"Yeah," said the other guard, "but what about that girl, Charley? Not the little one, but the one they just caught who got away? And the other stuff—pencil shavings in the library, the muddy sand outside the reptile exhibit—and how about that apple core?"

"That apple core could've been left there by one of the newspaper reporters or by a regular visitor—anyone, really," said Charley. "And we'd never have noticed the pencil shavings if it hadn't been for the break-in. The girl probably found her own way out; the cop said she was anxious to leave. I don't know about the sand, though. Maybe you have something there, but . . ."

The guards walked on, and Darcy scrambled out of the netting.

Brian was already sitting on the cot again. "That was stupid of us," he said. "I bet that sand's from us, from when we found that wet place. We should've cleaned our shoes . . ."

He poked Darcy sharply and dove to the floor, settling the cot on top of himself again as Darcy pawed her way back into the netting. She'd heard it, too: a faint scratching sound. Once she was hidden, though, she realized it wasn't in the hall outside. So it can't be the guards again, she decided.

There was a muffled thud and an equally muffled voice saying something like "Blast it!"

Then near the botanist's tent there appeared a mop of tousled red hair and then a plump, sweat-stained face.

"Numbles!" Darcy almost shouted, leaping to the balcony railing as Brian popped out from under the cot. "Sheesh, we thought you were the guards again!"

"Hi," said Numbles, grinning and running up the wooden steps to the balcony with two tattered and greasy paper bags. "That was a piece of luck! Have a doughnut."

He explained about George and Vincent, the duct, the loose window grating, and the water tank, and told them his theory about what the animal was. Brian explained about not finding the room in which Casey was a prisoner, and about the water exhibits being closed off and about not having time to explore them because of the ringing alarm. Darcy explained about being questioned by the police and the museum director.

"At least," said Brian, "we know more now than we did before." He began pacing, the way he often did when faced with what Holmes would have called "a three-pipe problem." Finally he said, "We know quite a bit more than we did, anyway. Numbles, I think your deduction about what the creature is might very well be right. Let's assume it is, anyway, for the moment, and that George and Vincent and maybe that guy who works for them—what's his name again?"

"Roderick," said Numbles.

Brian nodded. "Roderick. Let's assume that they're all after Champ." He looked grim. "What a crowd! Okay," he went on, "I think you're right that Roderick's being a taxidermist makes it look as if George and Vincent want to kill Champ to study his skull."

"Don't forget the *other* other guy," Darcy put in. "Belter, or Belton, or whatever. The circus one."

"Belton," Numbles supplied. "Right." He thought of Champ's sad, pleading eyes and cringed when he remembered reading that Nessie souvenirs—ashtrays, mugs, key chains—were big business near Loch Ness. Would there be Champie souvenirs if someone carted Champ around in a cage or put him in a zoo?

"Okay," Brian said, still pacing. "So we know we've got four enemies to watch out for: George, Vincent, Roderick, and Belton. They're not suspects, really, because so far they don't seem to have committed any crime. But it sure looks as if they want to, and it also looks as if we're the only ones who can prevent it. We also know that more scientists are coming on Tuesday to study Champ. We know Champ's got Casey, and it looks as if the only way we can get to her is through the tunnel, even if that pond is somehow connected to the water tank. We can't very well let the water out."

"As I said," Numbles told them, "I think Champ's holding Casey hostage. I think if we can get him back to his home . . ."

"Lake Champlain?" said Darcy. "Are you crazy?"

"I can call Uncle Fred," said Numbles quietly. "My uncle the herpetologist."

"Who lives," Darcy said, "in Arizona, if I remember right."

"And who," Numbles retorted, "might very well want to see the Lake Champlain monster if we could convince him that's what we've got. He might take a plane to Boston and maybe rent a van or something and drive us and Champ—and Casey, if Champ won't let her go—to Lake Champlain."

"School starts again on Tuesday," said Darcy, with a grin. "I'd be more than happy to miss it, even though I'll be campused if I'm back late."

"It won't be the first time," Numbles said dryly.

"Or the last," said Darcy cheerfully. "Wow, if we go to Lake Champlain, I won't get to school till Wednesday at least. How far is it from Lake Champlain to Maryland?"

"Far," said Brian abstractedly. "Do you really think," he said to Numbles, "that your uncle would come? Because obviously we can't get Champ to Lake Champlain without help."

"Yes, I think he'll come," said Numbles. "He loves traveling. He flies all over the world hunting for rare reptiles. And he'll be pretty curious if we say we think we've got the Lake Champlain monster. Especially when we tell him the scientists haven't figured that out yet."

"Okay," said Brian. "Let's try it. Only"—he paused—"let's really try to get Casey away from Champ ourselves. I agree we've got to take Champ to Lake Champlain, to save him from George and Vincent and Roderick and

Belton and maybe those other scientists, too. But we've also got to get Casey back home. That part would be a lot easier if we didn't have to take her to Lake Champlain, too."

"I agree," said Numbles.

"Me, too," said Darcy. "Okay, what's the plan?"

THE PLAN

THEY DECIDED THAT BRIAN would call Numbles's uncle, since Numbles was in danger of being seized by George and Vincent if they saw him again, and since Darcy was at risk of being seized by the police or the museum guards.

"How are we going to get your uncle into the museum, Numbles?" asked Darcy, when Numbles had given Brian his uncle's number.

There was a long awkward pause.

"Well," said Numbles finally, "I guess the only way, if the museum's still closed . . ."

"Which it probably will be," Brian reminded him, "till they find everything they're looking for."

"Wait," said Numbles, consulting his pamphlet. "It'll

be closed Monday anyway. It says here it's always closed on Mondays, except in the summer."

"So if we haven't been able to get Casey free and the museum's still closed, the best way in might be the window Kevin delivered the doughnuts through. Obviously he was able to open the window and that vent thing on the outside. So that just leaves the grating."

"Yeah," Darcy said, "but it's one thing to force a few bags of doughnuts between a loose grating and a window frame, but quite another to force a person through. Not to mention a monster, even a relatively small one. Your uncle's going to have to get the grating off."

"I'll call Kevin," Brian said. "He could meet Num's uncle and bring some tools."

"Will your uncle fit in the duct?" asked Darcy. "I mean, if it's as narrow as you said . . ."

Numbles stared at her. "You're right," he said dejectedly. "I don't think so."

"Will Champ fit?" Brian asked.

"I'm pretty sure he will. He's big, but he's sort of streamlined."

"We'll just have to get Champ and maybe Casey through the duct to the hall with the window, then," said Brian. "And hope George and Vincent aren't around. Or anyone else."

"Maybe," said Darcy, "I could create a diversion."

Brian and Numbles looked at her, and Numbles remembered the narrow escape she'd had not long before, creating a diversion when they'd been after a family of vampires.

"Maybe," said Brian. "If we really need it. But only if we really need it. There's no point in taking more risks than we have to."

"Okay," Darcy said impatiently. "Let's get going. Brian, you're going to call Kevin and also Num's uncle. How about I try again to get some fish for Champ? Numbles, then you and I can go back to the cave with it and see if we can get Champ to give Casey up. You could meet us back in the cave, Brian."

"Sounds good." Brian looked at his watch. "Ten o'clock. Does anyone know which ten it is? Morning or night?"

"And which day," said Darcy.

"Sunday," Numbles told them, "because of the doughnuts. Sunday morning."

"Doughnuts!" Darcy exclaimed. "We've got to get some to Casey. She must've finished her food by now. There's a sink in the SunLab, jars, too, so at least we can take her some water. I don't suppose the pond water would be safe to drink."

Brian shoved one of the bags over to her. "Okay," he said. "Darcy's right that we'd better get started. But remember, no unnecessary risks, especially you, Darcy. At least now we have a plan and we pretty much know what we're dealing with."

"You know what?" said Darcy. "I think a nice monster may be harder to handle than a mean one."

"We don't know for sure that he's nice," Brian said.

"No," Darcy agreed. "But if he wasn't, he would probably have done something awful to Casey right away."

"Holding people prisoner," Brian pointed out, "isn't exactly kind. Even if you don't hurt them, and they like you. We don't know how Champ's going to react when we try to get her away from him."

"We don't know how Casey's going to react either," Darcy pointed out. "She likes him, remember?"

"Could we get going?" Numbles asked. "I keep thinking of George and Vincent and that Belton guy. And Roderick, wherever he is. Let's not forget that Champ's in danger, much more danger than Casey."

"Casey," said Brian, "*could* be in serious danger if Champ feels threatened. We don't know what he'll do to her if someone goes after him. So be careful, you two." He stood up. "Let's go." Briskly he strode out of the rain forest exhibit, paused for a moment scanning the halls, and then made a dash for the escalator.

Darcy gave Numbles the doughnut bag, and led him

around the corner to the SunLab. Numbles got a sudden glimpse of bright light as she opened the door. In a few minutes she was out again, a jar of water in one hand and a green plastic bucket with something splashing in it in the other. "I got two fish," she whispered. "But I hate doing this. Giving him live ones."

"I know," Numbles whispered back as they hurried to the reptile exhibit and squeezed through the opening again. "But I don't see an alternative. Unless"—he waggled the paper bag—"he likes doughnuts."

"We could try," said Darcy. "And then if he does, we could put the fish in the pond."

"Or back in the SunLab," said Numbles.

They were in the cave tunnel now, walking rapidly along. Numbles realized they didn't seem to need the light anymore, now that they'd been there before, but even so, he was glad when Darcy pulled the guard's flashlight from her pocket. After all, if they did succeed in getting Casey away, she'd probably move a lot faster if she could see where she was going.

"I think it's here," said Darcy, stopping.

Numbles felt along the rough rock wall again and found the opening before he saw Brian's pile of pebbles. This time he poked his head in. Casey was curled up in the far corner, with the monster lying between her and the opening.

The monster seemed to be asleep.

"Pssst, Casey!" Numbles whispered. "Psssst! Over here!"

Casey moved a little, and sighed.

"Casey!"

She stretched and opened her eyes, yawning. "Huh?" she said.

"Over here! Quietly! Maybe," said Numbles, turning back to Darcy, "we won't need the fish at all."

But when he glanced back, he could see that Champ's head was up and bobbing warily, watching Casey.

Casey was shaking her head. "I don't want to go," she said. "Diney doesn't want me to, either."

"Casey," Darcy said patiently, "think a minute. You can't stay there forever. You'd starve to death. And your family would be even more upset than they are now."

"You'd miss school," Numbles put in. Darcy rolled her eyes.

"I hate school," Casey said stubbornly.

"Okay," Numbles said, "maybe, but you'd never see your friends again, or your mom and dad, or Kevin . . ."

"Or have Christmas," said Darcy, "or your birthday, or . . . or ice cream."

"Can Diney come, too?" Casey asked in a small voice.

"We'd like him to." Darcy winked at Numbles. "He has to go home, just the way you do, Casey. We think home for him is a big lake, Lake Champlain. Someone took him from it—kidnapped him—and we think he wants to go back. It's almost as if Diney kidnapped you to make the museum people take him home. Of course that's not possible—he's only an animal—but . . ."

"Anyway," said Numbles, "we think maybe we can get him to come out of the room now. We brought him some dinner. You, too, Casey."

He reached back and took the bucket from Darcy. "Hey, Champ," he said, dangling it carefully inside the opening. "Look—fish." Then he saw the problem. He couldn't get the bucket very far inside the opening. And if Champ went to it to get the fish, Casey would have to pass him in order to get out. It was obvious that Champ wouldn't stand for that. They'd have to distract him, at least at first.

"Casey," Numbles said quietly, "do you think you could take this bucket and put it down at the other end of the room? Then while Champ's eating the fish, you can scoot through the hole."

"He'll chase me," Casey said dubiously.

"That's okay," said Numbles, "as long as he chases you out. That'd be fine, because then he'd be out, too. Let's try it, huh?"

Casey, with one eye on the monster, sidled toward the opening and the bucket. But as soon as she moved, the monster put himself between her and the bucket, and batted at her with one of his flippers.

Looking more than a little startled, Casey ran back to the far corner.

"How about we throw a fish in?" suggested Darcy. "Then while Champ's eating it, Casey can run out."

"Okay," Numbles answered. "You throw, Darcy; you're the athlete. Casey!" he called. "Did you hear that?"

"Ye-yes," came the uncertain reply.

"As soon as he's busy with the fish," said Darcy, "you run out. Okay?"

"Okay," Casey answered, watching Champ warily now, as if she no longer quite trusted him.

Numbles withdrew the bucket from the opening. Darcy reached in for a fish, stepped away a little, drew back her arm, and let go.

But Champ caught the fish deftly in midair and gulped it down before Casey had even moved. Then he turned to her and enfolded her tightly in one front flipper. Casey whimpered softly.

"Sheesh," said Darcy. "Now what? We've got to feed Casey, too."

"Try the doughnuts," suggested Numbles. "Maybe Champ won't want them."

Darcy picked up the doughnut bag, took aim, called, "This is for you, Case," and threw.

Numbles and Darcy both gasped as Champ caught it—and then gasped again, for Champ had let Casey go. He sniffed the bag, dropped it in apparent disgust, and turned away.

Casey seized it and ripped it open.

While Champ was watching Casey gobble down the contents of the bag, Darcy was able to put the jar of water inside the opening. Casey was just able to snatch it before Champ grabbed her again.

"That's one thing accomplished, anyway," said Numbles. "Feel better, Casey?"

Casey nodded—and then there was a huffing and puffing back in the tunnel. Numbles and Darcy froze; Numbles held his breath—and then let it out again, relieved, as Brian emerged, saying, "It's all set. Your uncle's a prince, Num. He's taking the next plane. I gave him Kevin's number, and I called Kevin, too. I told him about Casey, and he got all sloppy for a minute, thanking us and stuff. I convinced him not to tell their parents yet, because they'd just send the cops barreling in, and then it would be all over for Champ. Kevin thinks the window will work, and he'll get the tools. Numbles, your uncle said he'd rent a van at the airport, and he said he'll bring some rope. He's all excited, by the way, and he agrees we should take Champ back to the lake. He also agrees we should try to get Casey away from

Champ first. The hitch is that your uncle won't be able to get here till around midnight. We've got to get to that hallway by then anyway—a little before then, really—and wait for him. We're going to have to be pretty careful, though. This place is bristling with cops again. I was nearly caught twice. Any luck on your end?"

"Nope, except we gave them some food." Numbles explained briefly, and they all looked through the opening again. Nothing had changed, except that Champ seemed more determined than ever to keep holding on to Casey. She seemed calm now, almost cuddling against him. "He's obviously not going to give Casey up easily," Numbles whispered. "Maybe we could lure him out with the second fish."

"Good," said Brian. Then he called, "Hey, Casey! Kevin says hi. Numbles's uncle is going to come and help us. We're going to try to get both you and Champ—um, Diney—out in a little while, when he's had time to get here."

"Suppose," said Darcy very softly, "Champ doesn't ever give her up?"

"We'll have to worry about that," said Brian, "when we get to Lake Champlain. Meanwhile, all we can do is wait for Num's uncle."

It was a long, boring wait. The three Monster Hunters took turns sleeping and watching, and whoever watched tried to keep Casey entertained by talking with her or telling her stories. The funny thing was, Numbles noticed during his third watch, that Champ seemed to enjoy the stories, too. Maybe it's just the sound of my voice, he thought, but the young monster put his head near the opening, and while Numbles—or Darcy or Brian—droned on, Champ's eyes stayed on the storyteller's face, his lids half closed.

"I'm running out of stories," Darcy said when it was almost time to leave. "And I'm starving."

"Kevin and Num's uncle are going to bring food," said Brian. "Sandwiches."

Numbles groaned. "Oh, please, let's not talk about food. It makes it worse."

"I'm past being hungry," Brian said. "I was starved for a long time, and my stomach hurt and everything, but now I feel fine. A little light-headed, but fine."

"You're probably in the last stages of starvation," said Darcy. "Like freezing to death, you know? Hey, Casey!" She went back to the opening. "How're you doing?"

"Okay," came a sleepy-sounding response.

"Only a few more hours, kid," said Darcy. "Then we're going to try to get you out again. Sound good?"

"Ummhmm. Diney, too. Remember he wants to go home. To that lake."

Darcy grinned and gave the boys a thumbs-up sign. Aloud she said, "Good girl. How's Diney doing?"

"He won't let me go," said Casey. "I think he's a little scared."

"Well, tell him we won't hurt him," Darcy called. "Tell him we're trying to help him. You know," she said, going back to Brian and Numbles, "it's okay to say we're going to lure him with the fish, sort of like luring a donkey with a carrot on a stick. But hadn't we better put him on some kind of leash in case he tries to bolt after we get him out?"

"Good idea," said Brian. "We could use our belts." He undid his, and Numbles did the same.

"They'll do for a collar," said Darcy, putting them together with her own, "and part of a leash, but they're not nearly long enough." She paused, frowning, and then shouted, "Vines! Those vines in the rain forest—we could use some of them! I'll go get some." Before the boys could stop her, she was sprinting down the tunnel.

Brian sighed. "She's right, of course. But if anyone sees her . . ."

Nobody did, and she was back in a few minutes with several thick, flexible stems, which she deftly tied together. "Girl Scout sailing camp," she explained. "They never got around to teaching us to sail, but they sure taught us a lot of knots. There. I took the vines from different places, so I don't think I left an obvious hole." She held up her handiwork. "That's a pretty good leash if I do say so myself. Strong, too." She yanked on it, demonstrating, and it held.

"Maybe we won't have to use the fish," Numbles said. "Maybe he'll let us put the collar over his head. Remember how he let me stroke him before."

"That's right," said Brian. "It's worth a try. Maybe if you talk to him, too, tell him another story."

"I'm out of stories," Numbles said.

"Make something up," Darcy suggested. "Or repeat one. I bet he won't mind."

"You tell the story, Darcy," said Brian. "Yours are the best ones, anyway. Go on, start one. And, Num, see if you can reach in and pat Champ. He's close enough to the opening, I think."

"Once upon a time," began Darcy, and Numbles put his hand into the opening. He found he could just reach Champ's back, so he stroked it gently, and pretty soon, Champ's big head came around. He stroked it, too, while Champ's eyes looked at him, first adoringly, then sleepily. . . .

"Now!" Brian whispered hoarsely when Champ's eyes had closed and his head had dropped. He handed Numbles the improvised collar, which had a length of vine already fastened to it.

Carefully, while Darcy's voice droned on, Numbles

slipped the collar over the sleeping creature's head and tightened it.

Brian pulled, and Champ slithered out of the opening. Numbles and Darcy grabbed Casey and pulled her free.

Then, as if he'd suddenly realized what was happening, Champ's eyes flew open and he bellowed.

A TIGHT SQUEEZE

THE THREE MONSTER HUNTERS froze at the horrible noise Champ had made. Then Numbles, realizing the sound had to have been heard throughout the museum, shouted, "Let's get out of here!"

Brian pulled on the vine leash, and Numbles pushed—Darcy was still holding Casey—but Champ wouldn't budge.

"The fish!" Numbles shouted at last. "We're forgetting the fish!"

Darcy kicked the green plastic bucket to Brian, who pulled out the now-motionless fish, and held it up in front of Champ.

Champ's eyes widened and his nose twitched.

"Good," Brian crooned softly. "Good monster. Come on—get the nice fish. Come on, come on!"

Champ turned away disdainfully.

"It's too dead," said Brian, and Numbles saw that Brian was breathing as shallowly as possible. "I don't blame him."

Suddenly Casey said, "Look at Diney," and pointed to the monster. He was stretching his neck and one flipper toward Casey.

"It's Casey he wants, still," said Brian briskly, "not fish. Okay, let's use that! Here . . ." He took Casey from Darcy and backed away down the tunnel, luring the monster with her, whispering, "It's okay, Casey. Remember, we're helping Champ go back where he lives."

"Diney," Casey corrected, but she also nodded solemnly.

Brian's plan worked. Slowly—painfully slowly, for Numbles could hear footsteps and confused voices through the tunnel walls—Champ edged forward, stretching, then lumbering, toward Casey. Brian edged backward, just as slowly, coaxing him on. Darcy and Numbles followed Champ, Numbles with the bucket. "We'd better not leave this behind," he said. "It'll look suspicious if anyone finds it."

"Fishy, you might say," remarked Darcy.

Numbles groaned, but Casey actually giggled.

At last they reached the mouth of the cave, where the pterodactyl still hung, and Brian made a shushing motion with his hand. "Wait here, you guys," he whispered. "I'll go check."

Numbles went ahead of Champ to guard Casey, and he and Darcy watched as Brian crept stealthily out of the cave and into the exhibit, moving the reticulate-collared lizard and the turtle gently aside. For a few moments, while Numbles listened anxiously to the commotion that Champ's bellow had obviously caused outside, Brian disappeared. But he came back quickly, saying, "We'll have to run for it; there are guards and cops all over the place downstairs. We'd better get away before they come up here. My guess is that they haven't figured out it was Champ who made the noise, since they don't think he's in the museum anymore. Come on; let's get going. Here, Num, I'll lead again!"

Still luring Champ with Casey, who now almost seemed to be enjoying herself, the little group, with Numbles and Darcy behind Champ, and Brian and Casey ahead of him, made its way through the broken panel and into the rain forest exhibit next door, where Numbles had emerged from the duct.

The sound of running footsteps and shouts echoed below them on the first floor. Numbles couldn't help but wonder where George, Vincent, Belton—and Roderick, if he was still around—were. Did any of them realize, he wondered, that it was Champ who'd made the awful noise?

What if he does it again?

But there was no time to think about that. "Come on, Num," Brian was saying. "You'd better go first, since you know the way."

Numbles moved to the head of the procession. He swept aside the vines covering the duct opening and squeezed through with the smelly fish bucket, followed by Brian and Casey. Then came Champ with Darcy close behind—and Champ stopped.

"Wait, Numbles!" Brian said in a loud, urgent whisper. "And, Darcy, you push!"

Darcy pushed, but Numbles, peering around Brian and Casey, could see the sudden terror in Champ's eyes. The monster had planted his flippers firmly under him, so they acted like four big brakes. His head bobbed up above the opening, and below it, and all around it, but never inside it; he seemed to have lost interest in Casey. Funny, Numbles thought, he didn't mind the room off the cave. But this is smaller; maybe that's the problem.

"He won't budge," came Darcy's voice from behind Champ.

Numbles moved back toward the opening, near Brian and Casey. "Come on, Champ," he called in what he hoped was a soothing voice. "Come on. Nothing's going to hurt you." He reached for the end of the vine leash, which was still dangling from Champ's neck, grasped it, and pulled. Darcy pushed some more, but Champ's head still bobbed frantically outside the duct opening, as if he was looking for a way around it.

"Brian," said Numbles, holding the leash as taut as he could, "see if you can grab his head and pull it in. Be careful, though," he added. "I don't think he'll bite, but you never know."

"Great," said Brian sarcastically, putting Casey down and grabbing Champ's neck. He lowered it firmly and as soon as his head was lined up with the opening, Numbles whispered, *"Now!"* Darcy pushed again, Numbles pulled quickly on the leash, and this time, at last, Champ followed. Brian let go of Champ's neck and moved ahead, keeping Casey just out of Champ's reach in case he got interested in her again.

There was a loud crash and a clatter just outside the opening.

"Sheesh," Numbles heard Darcy mutter, "what a mess! His tail's knocked down all the botany stuff!" And then he was too far along the duct to hear any more.

At first Numbles tried to crawl backward, so he could keep an eye on the situation, but that was too awkward, especially with the bucket, so he gave up and turned around, which there was barely room to do. Speed's got to be important, he thought, forging ahead and turning left without hesitation at the first intersection.

A moment later, though, he heard Brian say, "Whoa!"

Brian and Casey had made the corner all right, and so had Champ's head and neck, but the rest of Champ was wedged there firmly.

"Diney's stuck," said Casey, giggling. "He's stuck, he's stuck, he's stuck!"

"Shh, Case," Brian hissed angrily. "Do you want everyone to hear you?"

It was unusual for Brian Larrabee to be rattled, or to be beaten by a problem, but he seemed both rattled and beaten now.

Numbles edged toward him. "I think," he said, "that we've got to go back and start again."

"Yeah," said Brian. "So do I. But how do we get Champ to move backward? There's not enough room for him to turn around."

"True." Numbles thought quickly. "I've got another idea," he said at last. "Let me try something."

"Sure. Anything."

Numbles just barely managed to squeeze around Brian and Casey. Then he reached up and tentatively scratched Champ's head behind the little horns that stood up like ears.

Champ made a low, satisfied noise deep in his throat, and rubbed his head against Numbles's hand.

Casey giggled again. "He's purring!" she said. "Purring!"

Slowly, Numbles ran his hand down Champ's neck to his shoulder. Champ rubbed again.

Brian smiled. "I see what you're doing," he said softly. "Good man. It might just work."

Numbles nodded silently, and went on rubbing, lower on Champ's shoulder now, around to his back, down to his chest, then to his back again.

And Champ continued to rub against Numbles's hand ecstatically.

Finally Numbles found what he hoped was just the right spot, and he rubbed harder. Champ rubbed harder, too, stretching his body, catlike, toward Numbles. Each time he did that, his body lengthened and got thinner, the way a partly blown-up balloon would if someone stretched it. Brian, ahead of Numbles now, urged Casey forward and pulled on the leash—and at last Champ popped around the turn.

"Nice going, Num," said Brian, wiping his forehead.

They were about to set off again when they heard a faint high-pitched bleat, followed by a definitely female scream.

"Oh, no," said Numbles.

"Was that Darcy?" Brian's face had turned white.

"I've never heard her scream," said Numbles, "but it's sure a girl, and I haven't seen any other female people in here, except Casey, since the policewoman arrested the woman with the horrible fingernails, and that other woman, the one with the awful clothes, watched."

Casey whimpered. "I'm scared," she said. "I want Darcy."

It didn't take long for Darcy to straighten up the botanist's camp, putting lanterns and bowls in place and sweeping loose leaves back where they belonged. She was just returning some bags of leaves to their bench when she heard someone approaching, and she barely had time to dash under the steps to the balcony before a guard appeared.

He was walking slowly, searching methodically, as if he planned to cover every inch—no, every half inch, every quarter inch—of the museum with the proverbial fine-tooth comb. He didn't have a magnifying glass, but he might as well have, for he peered intently at every vine, every leaf, every object, even the lanterns and bowls that Darcy had so carefully put back.

Unfortunately one bag of leaves was still out of place. Darcy crossed her fingers, praying the guard wouldn't notice. After all, she reasoned, a museum guard couldn't possibly know exactly where every object was supposed to be.

This guard seemed to know. He frowned. He stepped back from the bag and viewed it from the left, then from the right, then straight on. He picked it up and turned it around, peered inside it, looked at its bottom—and finally replaced it, about two inches to the left of where it had been.

"Perfectionist," Darcy said disgustedly. Then she gasped, for he was staring at the vines and leaves around the duct entrance, and frowning.

"Diversion time," Darcy murmured, stepping out from under the steps. She crouched down in a sprinter's starting position, so she'd be ready to bolt, and then, after clearing her throat, she tried to scream.

What came out sounded more like a bleat from a sick sheep than a proper scream; Darcy hadn't had much practice. But her second attempt was terrific, so loud and high and clear that it startled Darcy herself.

It worked, too. The suspicious guard whirled and stared at her, then lunged—just as Darcy pushed off and tore out of the rain forest exhibit as if she were competing in the hundred-yard dash.

But instead of triumphantly crossing an imaginary finish line, she ran straight into the arms of a man in a tweed jacket.

"Well, well, well," he said nastily. "George, look what I caught!"

"We can't wait," Brian said decisively when the scream had died away. "We can't. She knows where we are; she's just got to find us if she can." He was still holding Champ's leash; Casey was in front of him, curled up unhappily on the duct floor, and Numbles had by now squeezed back into the lead position. Champ was still last in line, his eyes half closed in what looked to Numbles like stoic resignation, at least for the moment.

"I want Darcy," Casey said again, whining a little.

"So do we," Numbles told her. He looked at Brian. "She won't know which way to turn when she comes back in the tunnel," he said. "There are several branches."

"Can you mark them somehow?"

"I don't know. I've— Wait, I've got a pencil. I could write on the duct wall, maybe. But she'd never see it. We've got the flashlight, Brian."

"Can we barricade the wrong turns?"

"With what?"

"The fish bucket will do for this one," Brian said. Numbles set it down so it blocked the entrance to the wrong turn. "Phew!" Brian exclaimed. "It won't be long before someone smells it; I hope Darcy gets back before then. Now for the next turn. How many are there?"

"Three," said Numbles. "I alternated left and right at first—left, right, left. But the last left went to the tank, and the right came out in the rain forest. That was the left I just made. The next turn should be a left, too, and then a right. At least the other turns are wider than that first one was, if I remember okay. Maybe we could leave a note."

"Got any paper?"

Numbles searched his pockets. "A pencil, as I said. But I don't have any paper."

"Neither do I," said Brian. "Too bad. It was a good idea."

"The bucket," came a small voice, and both boys turned toward Casey.

"I wrote on a bucket last summer," Casey said proudly. "My name. On the beach, so no one would take it."

"Why not?" said Numbles. "Let's try it." He bent down and applied his pencil to the shiny surface of the bucket. He managed to scratch "LEFT HERE, THEN LEFT, THEN RIGHT" on it, but the lead was very pale and it didn't look as if the scratch marks would stay for long. "I'm not sure she'll even notice it," he said, "or be able to read it without a light."

"It's the best we can do, though," Brian said. "And Darcy's smart. If she has to find her way by trial and error, she'll just have to, that's all."

"It'll take her a lot longer, though," said Numbles as they made their way again through the duct. Champ still seemed resigned, and followed them doggedly with little urging, almost as if, Numbles thought, he's figured out we're trying to help him. Aloud, he said, "I hope Darcy makes it before we have to leave. I sure hope they didn't catch her again."

"So do I," Brian said grimly. "So do I."

Darcy rubbed her arm where Vincent had gripped it as he hustled her through the halls to the security chief's office again. He'd shoved her inside and left without showing his face, as if he didn't want to be seen. But the security chief himself was there, and he didn't look very friendly.

"You again," he said.

"I—I told you," Darcy sputtered. "I was here for the Camp-In. I know I should've come back after I went to the bathroom, but I got lost again, and then I fell asleep in that exhibit."

The security chief frowned and raised his eyebrows at an outrageously dressed woman sitting in a chair near his desk. She can't be a secretary, Darcy thought. Secretaries don't usually wear stirrup pants and tunics and have purple streaks in their hair. Also secretaries usually aren't around in the middle of the night. Maybe she's some kind of security person, disguised to look like a museum visitor for when she's here during the day. Some visitor, though!

"I checked the age of the last group of Camp-In kids," the woman said to the security chief. "They were Brownie Scouts, none of them older than eight." She turned to Darcy, and smiled.

Remind me, Darcy thought, not to wear orange lipstick when I grow up, if I wear lipstick at all.

"You look a lot older than eight," the woman said, still smiling.

Darcy was tempted to say, "I stayed back a lot in school," but she figured that might not work. "Okay," she answered, trying to look embarrassed. "You're right. I'm too old. But I *was* here at the Camp-In! You see, my little sister was going, and I'd never been to one, so I offered to help. I love the Science Museum," she said, smiling. "It's so perfect for kids. I mean there's so much to do and to play with and to learn, and I want to be a scientist myself when I grow up, so I . . ."

"What kind?" asked the chief.

"Huh?"

"What kind of scientist do you want to be?"

"Um—a—botanist."

The chief exchanged a glance with the woman, and rolled his eyes. "A botanist?" he said incredulously.

"What's *Hedera helix?*" the woman asked, leaning forward.

"English ivy," said Darcy promptly, silently thanking

her botany-loving science teacher for making her class label plant specimens with their Latin names.

Both adults seemed very surprised. The security chief sighed and said, "Okay." He turned to the woman. "I don't know quite what to make of this," he said, "but it doesn't look to me as if it has any connection to—er—to our other troubles. I think we can safely let her go. Frankly, I don't know what else to do with her." He turned back to Darcy. "I am going to phone your parents, who must be very worried, and then have Mrs. Pickering here, who's one of our security guards, escort you home . . ."

"My parents," Darcy interrupted, smiling sweetly and stalling for time and making details up as she went along, "are—um—away. I . . . my little sister—you know, the one whose Camp-In this really was—and I were supposed to be staying at a friend's house for the rest of the weekend, so I guess that's where she is now. My sister, I mean, but . . ."

"Then," said the chief, holding up his hand, "Mrs. Pickering will escort you to your friend's house. Everyone must be pretty worried about you by now." He reached for his phone. "What's your friend's name and number?"

Darcy gulped, but she thought quickly enough to say, "I don't know. She's my sister's friend. I just know her as—as Beverly. I think that's it—or maybe it's Brenda—or Barbara? Yeah, that could be it: Barbara. Anyway, isn't it kind of late to be phoning people?"

"Not if they're worried," said Mrs. Pickering dryly, standing up and glancing at the chief. "Surely you know where your sister's friend lives, even if you don't know her name. If you can't remember, maybe the police can figure it out. We'll go down to the station and see. If that doesn't work, I think we'd better track down your parents. I daresay you'll know *their* names and number and where they can be reached. Come along now."

Mrs. Pickering, gripping Darcy's arm far more tightly than Darcy thought necessary, led her out of the security chief's office, through the main lobby, and out one of the big front doors.

UNCLE FRED

"IS IT MUCH FARTHER, NUM?" Brian asked when they paused for a rest. He was obviously out of breath, despite his being an athlete.

"I don't think so." Numbles rubbed his arms. It seemed harder this time, pulling himself along the duct floor and pushing with his feet against its slippery surface. Champ didn't seem to be having much trouble, though.

Suddenly Numbles's hand bumped into something loose on the duct floor. The filter!

"Here we are," he said quietly to Brian, reaching ahead and lifting the latch. "We'll have to crawl over the filter. Wait, I'll go out and take it with me."

"They should be here by now," Brian said. "Kevin and your uncle. Here." He handed Numbles the flashlight.

"Can I come?" Casey piped up. "Please, can I? Diney, too?"

"Not yet," said Brian. "Soon."

"Soon," Numbles repeated. "Very soon, I hope." He squeezed through the opening and straightened up, glad to be able to do so, but wincing as pain shot through his body from muscles too long cramped. The pain eased quickly, though. He propped the filter up against the wall and shone his light around the narrow hall.

No one was there. Good, he thought, making his way quickly to the window.

But the window was tightly closed, and the grating was still intact.

"Blast it!" Numbles muttered, and went back to the duct. "No one," he said through the opening. "What time is it?"

"A little after twelve," said Brian. "They should be here, shouldn't they?"

"Yes. Maybe something went wrong."

"Or maybe your uncle's plane was late." Numbles heard Brian sigh. "We'll just have to wait, that's all," Brian said. "Come on back in the duct."

"That's okay," said Numbles. "I think I'll wait out here."

"Numbles, if someone comes, you might not have time to get back in."

"You're right," Numbles agreed reluctantly. Giving one last look around the empty hall, he climbed back into the duct, pulling the filter in as he went.

For a few minutes Darcy stood in the shadow of the museum, shivering in the autumn chill, trying to get her bearings and decide what to do next. It hadn't been hard to wrench free of Mrs. Pickering—Darcy knew a little karate—and elude her by running about half a block down the street and hiding under an elevated walkway that seemed to lead to part of the transit system. Mrs. Pickering had charged right on past her.

Now that Darcy was outside the museum again, she realized that she couldn't get back in through the doors. Okay, she reasoned, all I have to do is find the window Kevin and Num's uncle are going to use and go in that way.

Or just wait, since they ought to be here pretty soon.

Blowing on her cold hands and then jogging to keep warm, Darcy skirted the museum, trying to find the right window. Unfortunately there were several, all with vents and gratings over them; she had no idea which was the right one. So, she said to herself, I'd better keep going back and forth till I see Kevin and Num's uncle.

She jogged back to the front of the building. There wasn't much traffic, but there was enough light to see by. Only a couple of people were on the street, hurrying by on their private nighttime business. They didn't seem at all interested in Darcy—except that van, she thought nervously on her third trip back to the front of the museum. She'd noticed it the second time, without paying it much attention. But now it was pulling into the museum driveway slowly, almost as if it were following her.

She turned quickly, deciding to test it by running in the opposite direction to see if it turned, too. Just then a waving hand burst out of the front passenger window and a voice called quietly, "Darcy? Is that you?"

Of course, Darcy thought. What a dope I was not to realize. "Kevin!" she shouted happily. "Yes, it's me! Which window?"

"Around back. Wait. You might as well get in."

Kevin's hand went back inside, and the van pulled up to the curb. The passenger door opened, and Kevin pushed over closer to a large friendly-looking gray-haired man who, Darcy correctly guessed, was Numbles's uncle. He had a craggy but young-looking face despite his gray hair, and a grizzled chin that made him look as if he were trying to grow a beard or hadn't had time to shave.

"What are you doing out here?" Kevin asked when the introductions were over.

Darcy explained.

Kevin's uncle looked worried. "You say the animal's in the air-conditioning and heating duct?" he asked.

"Yes, along with Numbles and Brian and Casey," Darcy told him.

"I sure hope no one turns the heat on. It's pretty cold."

Kevin laughed. "Maybe that's because you're from Arizona, sir," he said politely, "and because of that trip to Africa you said you just came back from. It's cold, but it's not that cold. And I don't think they'd turn the heat on at night anyway. Most public buildings keep the heat off at night, even in the dead of winter. It decreases their fuel bills by as much as a factor of ten."

"Mmm," said Numbles's uncle dryly, "if you say so. But I'd hate to think of that animal's skin drying out too much."

How about Numbles's and Brian's and Casey's skin, Darcy wanted to ask, but she figured that might sound unnecessarily rude, so she didn't say anything.

"It's this window," Kevin said a moment later.

Numbles's uncle—Mr. Tangier, he said his name was—backed the van up onto a little grassy verge at the side of the drive, so that its rear door was as close to the window as possible. "It's a good thing this isn't in the front of the museum," Mr. Tangier said. "But we'd better hurry just the same. By the way," he went on, turning to Kevin, "I thought you said it was a basement window."

Kevin shrugged.

"The museum calls the bottom floor the basement," Darcy explained, a little puzzled herself. "The bottom floor where there are exhibits, anyway. But I guess maybe they have another basement under that, at least in the back. The ground's lower here than in the front," she added. "That might be why the window's high, even though it goes into a basement."

"Maybe so," said Mr. Tangier, turning off the ignition. "I guess ours is not to reason why, as the poem says."

The three of them got out, Mr. Tangier with a wooden box. "Burglar's tools," he said, grinning. "I had to break into a locked reptile house at a zoo once," he explained, setting the box down under the window, "to rescue a rare python that was being abused. But this is my first museum. My last, too, I hope."

Darcy, watching him reach up to the slatted wooden vent that covered the window, was pretty sure Mr. Tangier was enjoying himself tremendously.

"It's loose, all right," he said, wiggling the vent. "I can pull it open easily, just as you said, Kevin. But I'm going to have trouble with that grating, even though it's loose, too. The window's also a little high; our friends will have a bit of a drop when they come out. How did you get up to it, Kevin?"

"I didn't," Kevin answered. "I reached up with a couple of sticks. One to move the vents and the grating aside and the other to poke the doughnut bags in."

"I could climb up," Darcy offered, "on your shoulders or something."

"Me, too," said Kevin.

"Good idea," said Mr. Tangier, although he looked a little disappointed, as if he wanted to be the one to do the actual breaking in. As it was, he handed both tools and advice up to Darcy and Kevin as they took turns trying to remove the grating; it was a job that really required all three of them.

They were so intent on it, too, that they didn't notice the black car that pulled into the driveway and parked at one end, or the man who lurked in the shadows nearby.

It was very hard not to groan aloud, Numbles found, biting his lip every now and then when he tried to move yet another cramped limb and found it protesting by sending pain shooting along its every nerve. Brian and Casey were asleep. So was Champ. Numbles was fighting to stay awake; they'd agreed that one of them should listen for Kevin and Uncle Fred. He tried thinking of food—steak, potatoes swimming in gravy, chocolate cake, hamburgers oozing ketchup, fries, corn chips—but that made him hungry, so he stopped. Then his mind ran to thoughts like What if they don't come? and What if we have to go back? and What if George and Vincent and Belton and Roderick figure out where we are? and What if we die of starvation? That was too disturbing, so he tried whistling softly to keep his spirits up, but Brian woke instantly at that and said, "No whistling; someone might hear," so Numbles had to stop. He began reciting the Latin names of all the reptiles he could think of, starting with water snakes: *Natrix cyclopion cyclopian,* he began; *Natrix cyclopian floridana*—that went better. He was all the way to kingsnakes—*Lampropeltis triangulum elapsoides*—when he heard the noise.

It was a slight scraping sound, regular and metallic, as if . . .

As if someone were sawing at metal—sawing at the window grating!

"Brian," he whispered excitedly. "Wake up! I think they're here."

"Huh?" Brian said sleepily. He sat up, banging his head on the top of the duct. "Ouch, blast it! What?"

"I think they're here," Numbles whispered. "Listen."

In the silence that followed, Numbles heard the sound again. He could see that Brian did, too, for a wide grin slowly spread across his face. "All right!" Brian exclaimed. "I'll just crawl out and have a look"—and he disappeared.

While he was gone, Casey whimpered a little in her

sleep. Then Champ began to snore, and Numbles had a very hard time not laughing, partly in relief that Kevin and Uncle Fred were finally there, and partly because it was funny to think of a monster—even just an ordinary reptile—snoring. Luckily the noise wasn't very loud.

"Okay," Brian whispered, poking his head into the duct again. "It's them. And Darcy's with them, don't ask me why or how. She and Kevin are taking turns sawing the grating off. They're almost through it."

"Where's Uncle Fred?"

"He's there, too. They're using him for a ladder."

There was a low whistle.

"That means they're through," said Brian. "Come on, let's go. Hey, we're almost out of here!"

But getting out was easier said than done. First they had to wake Champ up, which proved to be harder than they'd expected. Then they had to quiet Casey, for as soon as they woke her up and told her it was time, she started squealing and shouting for Kevin. When they were out of the duct, she kept saying she wanted to take Diney home to show their parents before they took him to Lake Champlain.

"But, Casey," Darcy called desperately through the window, "he's *very* homesick. He's sorry to leave you, I'm sure, but he wants to go home now. Right, Numbles? Numbles knows all about—um—animals like Diney," she added.

"That's right," said Numbles. "Look at him, Casey. Doesn't he look as if he wants to go home?"

Luckily, Champ was eyeing the window and bobbing his head up and down.

Casey watched him a minute and then reached out to rub his neck. "Diney," she said softly, "do you really want to go home now?"

Champ turned, looking at her, and then, while Numbles and Brian watched tensely, Champ bobbed his head again, as if he were nodding.

"Okay," said Casey resignedly. "I guess you'd better go then." She pulled the big animal's head closer to her, planted a kiss on his cheek, and then let go. "Good-bye, Diney," she whispered, and moved aside.

"Come on, Champ," said Brian, tugging on the leash while Numbles, and then even Casey, pushed. Finally, when they'd gotten him under the window, they had to figure out how to get him up to it, and out.

He just stood there, still bobbing his head around.

"Holy Toledo," Numbles heard his uncle exclaim the first time Champ's head bobbed by the window and then shot out through it curiously. "Holy, holy Toledo!"

"See what I mean, Uncle Fred?" Numbles called.

"I sure do. I sure do. I . . . Wow, Num, what a find! What a specimen!"

"Do you think I'm right?"

"About Lake Champlain? Yeah. Yeah, I think you might be." Numbles heard his uncle laugh. "He— Good grief, Numbles, he's downright friendly."

"Pat him," called Numbles. "He really likes it. Scratch him between his horns."

Numbles heard his uncle laugh again, a deep chuckle, and he heard him murmur the way people murmur to dogs and cats and horses when they fondle them. He grinned.

"I hate to break this up," Brian said. "But how are we going to get Champ out of here? And Casey. Let's get her out first."

"Yes, me first!" cried Casey. "Maybe Diney's scared. He'll go if I go."

"Atta girl," Darcy called from outside. "Come on. We'll catch you."

"Boost her up," called Uncle Fred, and he received her in his arms almost as soon as they did. Numbles couldn't help smiling when she squealed, "Kevin, Kevin, here I come!"

"Now for the hard part," came Uncle Fred's voice from the other side of the window. "I see you've got a leash on him. And I've got some rope. Wait, I'll just go get that. I've got some fresh fish, too."

Uncle Fred's voice faded.

"Darcy?" Brian called. "You still there?"

"Yeah," came Darcy's voice. "Kevin, too."

"What happened? How did you get outside?"

Darcy told them, and by the time she had finished, Numbles heard Uncle Fred say, "Here." A moment later Darcy appeared at the window with a heavy rope. "Put this under his flippers back and front," she instructed. "Mr. Tangier says that if all else fails maybe he can fasten the rope to the van and pull him out. Hey, Champ," she said, waving a large freshwater perch, "look what I've got!"

Champ straightened up as Darcy tempted him with the fish, so it wasn't hard to slip the rope around him, under his back flippers, along his back, and under his front flippers.

"Come on, Champie," coaxed Darcy. "Come on and get the nice fish. Come on!"

Her voice faded a bit as Champ's head and then, wonder of wonders, his front end, disappeared out the window. Uncle Fred must have Darcy on his shoulders, Numbles thought, and must be walking away.

Then from outside Kevin shouted, "Push from behind, we've almost got him!"

The rope tightened. Numbles and Brian ran around to Champ's back end, which had begun to rise a little off the floor. They pushed, and then suddenly, as if over-balanced by greater weight in the front, Champ's back end flipped up and the rest of him toppled out the window.

There was the sound of a car engine revving. Brian seized Numbles, saying, "Up with you." When Numbles grabbed the sill, Brian pushed him from underneath and he, too, toppled out the window—and onto Champ, who was now in the back of the van, contentedly munching on the perch and looking none the worse for wear. Casey, one hand firmly clutching Kevin's, was devouring a peanut butter and jelly sandwich and chattering to him excitedly. Uncle Fred handed Numbles a sandwich, too, just as Brian tumbled into the van. He must've chinned himself to get up to the window, Numbles thought, gratefully biting into the soft bread and savoring the tangy taste of the peanut butter, the sweet gooiness of the jelly. Wish I could do that!

And then Kevin and Casey climbed in, too. The van shot away from the museum and out onto the streets of Boston.

"First stop," said Mr. Tangier, "the Rogoffs'. Next stop, Lake Champlain."

The black car pulled away from the curb, and a man in baggy green cords darted out of a doorway, hopped into a small pickup truck, and sped after both it and the van.

HEADING NORTH

NUMBLES DIDN'T REALIZE how tired he was till Uncle Fred got out of the city after dropping Kevin and Casey off, and settled down to an even pace on the highway north. There was room on the front seat for two people besides Uncle Fred, but Numbles had elected to stay in the back with Champ and Brian's and Darcy's packs, which Kevin had brought. It was dark back there, windowless, except for the opening to the front seat, and soon Numbles propped himself up against Champ's flank, closed his eyes and fell asleep, soothed by the gentle motion of the van.

The sky was just getting light when the gentle motion stopped, and Numbles woke up, rubbing his eyes sleepily. Champ, he could see in the dim light coming from the front windows, was asleep, with his back legs and flippers folded under him, like a large, ungainly dog. Carefully, Numbles moved away from the animal's side and leaned into the front seat. "Where are we?" he asked.

"Vermont," said Brian. "We're just about at Lake Champlain. Your uncle's headed for the shore so we can see how Champ reacts."

"Good morning, Numbles," Uncle Fred said, looking at him in the rearview mirror. "Sleep well? How's our prehistoric friend?"

"Yes, I did, and he seems okay," Numbles replied. "By the way, thanks for coming and everything. And for the sandwiches."

"Don't mention it. Darcy, if you reach under the seat, I think you'll find a bag with some muffins in it, and if you're really lucky, there'll be a thermos of hot chocolate as well."

Darcy reached down, and a moment later she handed Numbles two muffins and a plastic cup of steaming chocolate. He scarfed them down in mere seconds.

"What if Champ doesn't react to the lake?" asked Darcy.

"I think he will," said Uncle Fred. "I can't guarantee it, of course, but . . . well, most creatures react to their native habitat. And I'm pretty sure you're right that this is Champ's. Last month," he went on, "when I was in

Africa, I had to get some baby crocodiles away from a poacher. They went bananas when I got them to the river where they'd been born. The thing to remember about reptiles is that even though they're not long on brains, bless 'em, they've got plenty of good old-fashioned instinct."

Uncle Fred, Numbles tried to tell himself, does know what he's doing when it comes to most known reptiles and amphibians. But I sure hope he knows what he's doing when it comes to ones that nobody's identified.

"There's a ferry here," said Uncle Fred, making a sharp left, "so I kind of hope this isn't where Champ wants to get out. I'd just as soon no one saw him. Also . . ." He glanced in the rearview mirror again. "I'm afraid we're being followed."

"What?" Numbles and Brian said almost simultaneously. Brian reached for the window handle on his side, but Uncle Fred quickly said, "No, don't look. I don't think they know we know. Just act normal."

Darcy laughed. "Oh, sure—normal! With a one-hundred-pound monster in the back."

Uncle Fred laughed, too. "You know what I mean. Num, you keep an eye on our friend, and the rest of us will pretend we're going to take the ferry."

"Are we?" asked Brian.

"Not unless we have to," said Uncle Fred. "My plan

is to explore this side of the lake, and then cross over and explore the other side."

"Champ was found in the Adirondacks, though," Numbles pointed out. "Wouldn't it make more sense to start on the New York side of the lake?"

"He was found in a cave," said Darcy. "Maybe we should be looking for caves."

"Looking for a cave in the Adirondacks would be like looking for that needle in the haystack people are always talking about." Uncle Fred rubbed his grizzled chin; Numbles could hear the rasping sound his hand made against the stubble. "But you're right about starting on the New York side. I suppose that would make more sense. Maybe we'll take the ferry after all."

"Nope," said Darcy a moment later when they stopped at the shore. There was a Closed sign hanging over the larger sign that gave the ferry's schedule and its rates. Then she said, in a much quieter voice, "Look."

Pulling up behind them was a black car with what looked like two men in it—or was it three? Numbles couldn't see too clearly from his position in the back.

"Act natural." Uncle Fred pulled a curtain across the space between the front seat and the back of the van. "I'm going to leave, but at a normal speed. I think I'll even wave. You, too, kids. Let's all wave. We're happy tourists," Numbles heard Uncle Fred say as the van turned, pulling out, "here for the long weekend; this is our last day, though—got to get you kids back to school. I'm your uncle," he said, obviously addressing Brian and Darcy. "I'm everyone's uncle," he sang merrily, "everyone's uncle. Hi, there, good morning!" he shouted—to the men in the car, no doubt, Numbles thought in admiration. "Nice day, isn't it?" Numbles felt the van swerve suddenly.

"What was that?" he asked.

"A little pickup truck," said Uncle Fred. "Behind the black car. I was trying to get out of its way."

"The truck," Brian observed, "had Vermont plates."

"So it's probably local," said Darcy.

"Probably," said Brian. "Except I think it's been in the city recently."

Numbles pulled the curtain open again. "How come, Holmes?" he asked Brian.

"Elementary, my dear Watson," said Brian. "There was a white paper on the dashboard that looked an awful lot like a parking ticket."

"Good work," said Uncle Fred. "You really *are* a detective, just as Numbles said. And Holmes was the best, even if he was fictional. You can't go wrong, modeling yourself on him. In fact, I knew a fellow in Madagascar once, who . . . but that's too long a story. We'd better concentrate on this 'little problem,' as I think Holmes might term it, for now." He glanced into the mirror again. "How's our friend, Num? Any reaction to being near the lake?"

"I don't know," Numbles said with considerable embarrassment. "I didn't look at Champ. I was thinking about the car that was following us."

"*Is* following us," Darcy corrected. "It's pretty far behind, but it's the same car. The black one."

"And," said Brian a moment later, "it looks as if the truck's following it. Again pretty far behind."

"Of course," said Uncle Fred, "as I guess our friend Holmes might point out, there's no place else for a car to go on this road but the way we're going. We'll know more when there's a turn. Like right here." He swung the van down a side road.

Numbles was aware of all this only dimly; he was watching Champ, whose head was up now and whose eyes were wide open. He was bobbing his head slowly, and his nostrils were ever so slightly flared; he was sniffing.

"Uncle Fred," Numbles said quietly when he'd watched this for a few seconds, "I think Champ's interested."

Uncle Fred turned around and looked over his shoulder. Then he laughed; Champ's head had shot out toward the windshield, and he peered eagerly ahead. "I think so, too," he said, patting Champ's head. "Good boy, Champie," he said. "But I don't think you'd better stay like this; if someone sees you, it'll be all over. Num, see if you can get him back, okay? We'll take the next road down to the shore."

In a few minutes Uncle Fred turned left again, and then made another left. When they reached the water, Champ's head bobbed faster and he made a low noise in his throat—his "song," Darcy called it.

"Should we let him out?" Numbles asked.

"I don't think so." Uncle Fred stopped the van and turned around, studying Champ. "I don't think we dare to in broad daylight. Hi, Champie," he said, reaching up to stroke the animal. "Have we found it, old son? Hmm?"

Champ shot his head forward again, thrusting it diagonally to the right over and over again and "singing."

"Mr. Tangier!" Brian exclaimed. "I think he's giving us directions!"

Uncle Fred watched him. "If he is," he said slowly, "he's telling us to go northwest, which could mean the other side of the lake—the New York side, as you said, Num."

"Don't look now," said Darcy, "but that black car's here again."

"Drat!" Uncle Fred turned around again. "Okay, hang on."

This time he sped along the road, jouncing over ruts and kicking up dust as he went. From the speed, Numbles was pretty sure the black car was still following.

"Chimney Point," said Brian waving a map, "is the next crossing place. It looks as if there's a bridge there, and some old fort or other, and a park. Crown Point, it's called." He turned around. "Crown Point?" he said to Champ, as if the creature understood English. "That mean anything to you?"

But Champ was just lying quietly again, his eyes half shut, and his song silent.

In a while, though, as they got closer to their goal, Champ became alert once more. In fact, it was all Numbles could do to keep him from poking his head forward. "If it weren't for that blasted car following us," said Uncle Fred, "or the chance of another car's going by and seeing that we've got the Lake Champlain monster in here, I'd say let him look." He shook his head as if in disbelief. "Whoa," he said. "Did you hear that? We've got the Lake Champlain monster in here! Not too many people can say that, kids. Too bad we don't at least have a camera. But . . ." Champ's head bobbed dangerously close to the windshield. Uncle Fred chuckled. "Hey, I'm sorry, Champie, old son," he said, giving the monster's head a little push, "but we're trying to protect you."

"Here's the road to the bridge," Darcy said suddenly,

looking outside and then pointing to the map. "You turn left here."

"Left it is." Uncle Fred swung the van around.

They drove through farmland for a while, past autumn-browned fields and cows that looked as if they'd rather be inside a warm hay-filled barn than outdoors trying to find the last few blades of edible grass. Some houses had plastic pumpkin-faced bags of leaves outside, left over from Halloween, and bunches of cornstalks. Most had big woodpiles nearby.

"Pulling themselves in for the winter," observed Uncle Fred. "I'd forgotten what it was like to live back east in the cold. Brrr! No thanks! I'm a bit like a reptile myself, I guess—I take on the temperature of my surroundings. Whoops! Hang on!"

Uncle Fred maneuvered the van around a sharp curve, and they found themselves facing a high bridge, with a closed historic monument and park to their left. A sign proclaimed that just over the bridge was a place called "Historic Crown Point."

"Not as well known as Fort Ticonderoga just to the south," remarked Uncle Fred, "but I've heard it was pretty important even so. There's a little bay here, with a funny name—Bulwagga—and there was a fort here that the French and English fought over in colonial times. I did some guidebook reading on the plane," he explained, "and I . . ."

"Look out," said Darcy suddenly. "Here they come! Watch it! Get Champ back!"

Numbles grabbed for Champ's head, which had shot forward again, even more excitedly than before, just as Brian shouted, "Gun it!"

As the van sped onto the bridge, Numbles caught a glimpse in the sideview mirror of the black car bearing down on them fast.

CONFRONTATIONS

THE VAN CAREENED OVER THE BRIDGE, with Uncle Fred cursing under his breath as he drove. Numbles found himself holding on to Champ's neck as the van swayed dizzily.

"Hang on," said Uncle Fred when they were on the New York side of the lake. "I'm going to swing into this park and then try to double back out again before he has time to turn around. Hang on!"

As he said that, the van screeched to the right and seemed to be making a circle. It seemed to be in danger of tipping over, too, Numbles thought, as he held on for dear life. Champ's face came close to his for a moment, and Numbles could see that he was frightened, so he put up his hand and stroked him gently. "It's okay," he said softly. "You're almost home. At least I think you are. I hope you are!"

Then Numbles felt the van stop.

For a second everything was quiet. Then Numbles heard an unpleasantly familiar voice—Vincent's—saying, "You've led us quite a chase, whoever you are, but we've got you now. Out of the van. Let's go. Roderick, get off your lazy tail and open the door for the man. It's bad enough that you tried to quit on us. But now that we've found you, you're darn well going to work. Move!"

Numbles fought down the temptation to look. As it was, he had just time enough to reach up and pull the curtain closed before he heard the van's two front doors open and the sound of his uncle and Brian and Darcy getting out.

"All we want," he heard George saying with exaggerated calm, "is the animal. We know you've got it. Look, we're scientists—well, two scientists and a taxidermist—not crooks, for Pete's sake. We don't want to harm you."

"But we will," Vincent said menacingly—so menacingly that Numbles was sure he had a gun—"if you don't hand over the beast, and fast. Right, Roderick?" Numbles heard a sharp noise that sounded suspiciously like a rifle being cocked.

"Oh, er . . . yes, right," said a scared-sounding third

voice. "Right. We—er—we have . . . that is, my—my employers have . . ."

"Oh, shut up, Roderick," Vincent said disgustedly. "I almost wish we *hadn't* found you hiding under those stuffed birds, coward that you are!"

"Gentlemen, gentlemen," Numbles heard Uncle Fred say quietly, "maybe we can talk this over like civilized people. Everyone and everything in this world has a price, you know. Let's just have a seat someplace comfortable and see if we can work this out."

Oh, no, Numbles thought, astonished and angry. Is Uncle Fred going to *sell* Champ? How could he?

But it sure seemed like it; at least he heard the four men move away, heard a car door open and shut, and then heard a quiet click as the van's back doors opened and Brian and Darcy climbed in.

"Have they got a gun?" Numbles asked.

"Yes," Brian answered breathlessly, "two, in fact—a rifle and the tranquilizer gun Darcy and I heard them talking about back in the museum. They're using the rifle now, but your uncle's being pretty cool. And I don't think they saw Darcy and me get out. In any case, it's not us they care about. I think your uncle's trying to give us time to get away with Champ, Num."

"But we can't drive!" exclaimed Numbles.

"I think I can," said Darcy. "I tried driving my dad's

car once when I was eleven, and I nearly wrecked it, but ever since, I've paid a lot of attention to how people do it." She moved the curtain aside and looked at the dashboard. "The keys are still in the ignition," she announced. "We've got to hurry, whatever we do. So let's do the only thing we can—get Champ out of here." She climbed into the front seat, turned the key, and a moment later they were tearing out of the park . . .

Only to be stopped at the park entrance by the little pickup truck.

"Blast and double blast!" said Darcy furiously, stalling as she wrenched the van sharply to one side. But the truck swung around faster, till its rear bumper was right against the van's back door. Before Darcy had time to start the van again, a man—the man in baggy cords—Belton, Numbles realized, his heart sinking—had pulled down the pickup truck's back gate, yanked the van's back door open and was pulling on the rope and the vine leash, both of which were still attached to Champ.

"Come on," Belton said impatiently to Numbles. "There's no time to explain. But I'm friend, not foe. Help me get him out of here."

For a moment Numbles couldn't move. He just stared at Belton, as did Brian and Darcy.

"Look," shouted Belton, still tugging, "I'm Dr. Jeffrey

Belton, a cryptobiologist, which means roughly that I study creatures that no one believes exist."

Whoa, thought Numbles, remembering the man had called himself that back when the cops had led him away. So that's what that is! I wish I'd known that when he said it to the police! He sure doesn't sound as if he's interested in Champ just as a curiosity, as that creep Vincent said.

"If you've guessed that this is a Lake Champlain monster," Dr. Belton was saying, "you're right. I'd dearly love to keep him for a while to study and photograph him, but as you may have noticed, he's in grave danger right now, and the best thing we can do is return him to where he belongs. That ought to be very near here, unless I miss my guess. I've got a boat down in Port Henry; I'm hoping we can get to it and out on the lake with the monster before those three creeps figure out where we've gone. Will you give me a hand?"

"He's on the level, I think," Brian said decisively, hopping out of the van. "Besides, he's our only hope."

Darcy followed Brian, and before long, the four of them had managed to transfer Champ to the back of the truck. Dr. Belton threw a tarpaulin over the open part of the truck and buttoned it down securely. "To keep out prying eyes," he said, opening the truck door for the three Monster Hunters. "Don't worry; it's got air holes."

A few minutes later they were squeezed together in the truck's front seat, more or less on one another's laps as they sped along the road on the New York side of the lake, toward Port Henry.

"I'm sorry I had to follow you," Dr. Belton said, "and that I couldn't introduce myself earlier. But there just didn't seem to be any opportunity, especially after the cops finally believed me and let me go, along with that woman reporter they thought was working with me."

"So," said Numbles, "she really was a reporter."

"Yes," said Dr. Belton. "And I'm not sorry her sweatsuited editor pulled her off the story. She was getting a little too close to the truth for comfort. I've been studying the Lake Champlain monsters for more than twenty years," he went on, glancing every so often in the rearview mirror as if checking to see if the black car was following them. "And when I read a description of the animal that was being exhibited at the Museum of Science, I was pretty sure what he was, so I hightailed it to Boston to see. Then when I found out all those scientists were coming to poke at him, I got worried. And when I realized those two creeps and their taxidermist were trying to capture the monster, I got really worried. We've got official rules in New York and Vermont protecting Champ, but I don't think the people who found him have ever heard of them, and since they found Champ in a cave, I guess they figured he couldn't be what I think he is."

"What *do* you think he is, Dr. Belton?" Numbles asked.

Dr. Belton smiled. "I subscribed to the plesiosaur theory for a long time," he said. "But now that I've seen Champ close up, I don't think he's anything we've ever heard of." He looked in the mirror again. "Still no one behind us?"

"No one," said Darcy. "I've been watching. I hope Mr. Tangier's all right."

Numbles said fervently, "So do I."

"Anyone who can handle crocodiles," said Brian, "ought to be able to take care of himself." But it was obvious he was worried, too.

"We'll go back and check on him," said Dr. Belton, "as soon as we get Champ back where he belongs. But I already gave the police a call." He pointed to the dashboard, where Numbles now saw what he took to be some kind of shortwave or citizens band radio apparatus. "Anyway, two of those three guys looked pretty scared, and the one with the rifle didn't seem any too sure of himself once your uncle stood up to him. By the way, look."

Dr. Belton pointed to the right and slowed down in front of a big reddish brown sign, like a huge decorative screen with three sections. It was headed CHAMP SIGHTINGS IN BULWAGGA BAY AREA & VICINITY. Beneath the heading was a list of names and dates. The cut-out wooden figure of a cartoon-style light green Lake Champlain monster peered cheerfully over the top of the sign.

"There've been more sightings around here than anywhere else," Dr. Belton explained. "That's why I think this would be a good place to put him back in." He looked in the mirror again. "Still no one?"

"No one," said Darcy.

"I wish we knew if Uncle Fred was all right," said Numbles.

"Maybe the police have gotten there by now," Brian said.

"I bet they have." Dr. Belton slowed down as he entered a small, hilly village. "But if they haven't, I don't think those guys will bother with your uncle. I think as soon as they find out we've got the monster they'll let him go and come after us."

They drove through the village in tense silence and then turned to the right toward the lake, where there was a marina. "Not too many boats here now," said Dr. Belton as he backed the truck carefully toward a cement boat-launching ramp that extended out into the lake, "but in the summer, there are regular traffic jams. Now then." He stopped the truck and got out. "This is going to be a little tricky. Thank goodness no one's around. Can you imagine the fuss there'll be if anyone sees what we're doing?"

Numbles put an anxious hand on his arm. "I just thought of something," he said. "What if Champ's too young to live in the lake? What if Lake Champlain monsters are basically land animals when they're young and water ones when they're grown up, sort of the reverse of amphibians? What if Champ hasn't got the right kind of breathing apparatus yet?"

"You saw him swimming in that tank, Num, remember?" Brian reminded him. "You said he seemed pretty happy there."

"Yeah, you're right," Numbles said, relieved. "Okay."

"If he can't last long underwater, we'll probably know it pretty quickly," said Dr. Belton. "And we can pull him out—or he'll come out. Okay. Now I'm going to scootch my boat up as close as possible to the ramp. My plan is to load Champ onto it, take him out to deeper water, and—hello!"

There was a thrashing noise from the back of the truck, and suddenly Champ's head and long neck broke through the tarpaulin. His head was bobbing excitedly, and he was sniffing hard, taking in great gulps of air. His eyes, Numbles swore afterward, looked happy, and . . .

"He's singing again," said Darcy softly. "Listen."

Sure enough, from deep in Champ's throat came what could only be described as a happy song.

And then an extraordinary thing happened. While all four of them watched, transfixed, Champ slithered out of the truck and lumbered over to Numbles. He put his head down close to Numbles's and very softly brushed against his cheek.

Dr. Belton quickly removed the rope and the vine leash.

Champ, with a final bob at all of them, waddled over to the ramp and slid silently down it into the water.

For a few minutes, they could see his large form, and then they could see only his neck and bits of his body—"like the hoops they show in pictures of sightings," said Dr. Belton, his voice full of wonder, "but smaller, since he's still so young."

"But not so young," said Numbles in relief, "that he's not ready to live in the water."

Finally, just as the harbormaster came tearing down to the boat landing, shouting excitedly and waving his arms, Champ disappeared.

HOMEWARD BOUND

WHEN THEY WERE ALL BACK near the bridge with Uncle Fred, who seemed only a little the worse for wear, Darcy grinned at Numbles and Brian. "I guess we really did get our monster this time."

"Or kept the wrong people from getting him," said Brian. "Thanks to you, Dr. Belton, and you, too, Mr. Tangier."

The police had indeed come, Uncle Fred had explained, but before they'd arrived, Uncle Fred had wrenched the gun away from Vincent and held him, George, and Roderick prisoner with it. "I figured you guys had gone off with Champ," Uncle Fred said, "so I wanted to give you as much time as possible. It's a good thing I didn't know about Dr. Belton, though, or I'd have panicked, thinking he'd kidnapped the lot of you."

The police, Uncle Fred told them, had let George and Roderick go, reluctantly, for there didn't seem to be anything criminal they could charge them with—"just attempted everything," Uncle Fred said—but they'd taken Vincent, with his gun, in for questioning. "I doubt he's going to say anything about the Lake Champlain monster, though," Uncle Fred said with a grin. "If he does, they'll probably think he's off his rocker."

"Then you're not going to press charges against him?" Dr. Belton asked.

"No, indeed." Uncle Fred smiled. "If I did, we'd risk having the whole story come out, and then the lake would be swarming with people trying to see Champ."

"Thank you," said Dr. Belton, grinning and shaking Uncle Fred's hand. "As it was, I had a hard time convincing the harbormaster in Port Henry that he must have seen a trick of sunlight on the water instead of Champ."

Not much later that Veterans Day afternoon, Dr. Belton took the three Monster Hunters and Uncle Fred to the Amtrak station in Port Henry to wait for the train that would take Brian home to New York City. As soon as he left, Numbles and Darcy were going back to Vermont in the van with Uncle Fred. Numbles and Brian would both be home in time to go to school on schedule the next morning. But Darcy, who'd called her parents in Vermont and her school in Maryland, would be a day late, as she'd predicted. "So what if I'm campused for a couple of weeks?" she'd said cheerfully. "As long as they don't keep me from playing hockey, I'll be fine."

"What are you going to do about this sighting, Belton?" asked Uncle Fred curiously as they waited for the train.

"I'm not sure," he answered, "besides trying to go on protecting the lake monsters from people like George and Vincent and Roderick. Probably nothing, except use the knowledge I've picked up to continue looking for the monsters so I can study them in the field. I'm kind of torn about that, though. Maybe it'd be better to give up and just leave them undisturbed."

Maybe it would be, Numbles thought later, riding back to Vermont with Uncle Fred and Darcy. He looked out the window as the van left the lake behind. Its surface was smooth and blue—quiet, beautiful, and mysterious.

Yes, Numbles said to himself. I'm sure it would be.

ABOUT THE AUTHOR

NANCY GARDEN graduated from Columbia School of Dramatic Arts and has a master's degree from Columbia Teachers College. No matter what other kind of job she's had—actress, lighting designer, teacher, editor, book reviewer—she's always written, starting with a story that she wrote for fun at the age of eight. Story ideas, she says, can come from anyplace. One of her first books—called *Vampires*—was sparked by a can of cat food labeled DO NOT TOUCH—PROPERTY OF COUNT DRACULA. That book, and the research she did for it, eventually led to the Monster Hunters Series. Titles in that series are: *Mystery of the Night Raiders, Mystery of the Midnight Menace, Mystery of the Secret Marks,* and *Mystery of the Kidnapped Kidnapper*, all available from Minstrel Books. Ms. Garden lives in Carlisle, Massachusetts, and West Tremont, Maine, with a friend and a variety of cats and dogs.